Nobody c...

Of ...

Dear Reader,

I love writing FORBIDDEN FANTASIES for Blaze, and so getting the chance to write three in a row is a real treat!

Seven years ago, spurred on by their father's wedding, a bottle of champagne and a serious case of lust for their new stepmother's gorgeous sons, Adair, Piper and Nell MacPherson each wrote down their most secret sexual fantasies about their "ideal" man and buried them in a stone arch on their family's estate. Then they forgot all about them. Almost.

Now, one by one, the Sutherland triplets, Cam, Duncan and Reid, are being drawn back to Castle MacPherson, not only by the erotic fantasies penned all those years ago, but also to right a wrong and restore a stolen bride's long-missing dowry to its rightful owners.

I hope that you enjoy Cam and Adair's story, *No Risk Refused*, and that you will look for *No Holds Barred* in September and then *No Desire Denied*. All three books feature an amazing dog named Alba, who currently resides at the Northeast Animal Shelter in Salem, Massachusetts, but is waiting for her forever home. I hope you fall in love with her just as I did.

For news on my future releases, visit www.carasummers.com. And for more information on the Northeast Animal Shelter and the Blaze Authors' Pet Project, visit www.blazeauthors.com/blog.

May all your forbidden fantasies come true!

Cara Summers

NO RISK REFUSED

BY
CARA SUMMERS

First published in Great Britain 2012
by Mills & Boon, an imprint of Harlequin (UK) Limited,
Eton House, 18-24 Paradise Road, Richmond, Surrey TW9 1SR

© Carolyn Hanlon 2012

ISBN: 978 0 263 89738 8
ebook ISBN: 978 1 408 96926 7

14-0812

Harlequin (UK) policy is to use papers that are natural, renewable and recyclable products and made from wood grown in sustainable forests. The logging and manufacturing processes conform to the legal environmental regulations of the country of origin.

Printed and bound in Spain
by Blackprint CPI, Barcelona

Was **Cara Summers** born with the dream of becoming a published romance novelist? No. But now that she is, she still feels her dream has come true. And she owes it all to her mother, who handed her a Mills & Boon novel and said, "Try it. You'll love it." Mom was right! Cara has written over forty stories for Blaze, and she has won numerous awards including a Lifetime Achievement Award for Series Storyteller of the Year from *RT Book Review*s. When she isn't working on new books, she teaches in the writing program at Syracuse University.

To my sons, Kevin, Brian and Brendan.
As you've grown into fine young men, I've seen
you do everything you can to protect and cherish
the ones you love. In short, you inspire my heroes.
Thanks! I love all three of you.

And special thanks to the best editor in the world—
Brenda Chin. You have once more pulled one of
my stories out of the darkness and into the light.

Prologue

THUNDER CRASHED AND lightning ripped through the sky while rain lashed at the stone arch over Eleanor Campbell MacPherson's head.

Perfect, she thought.

It was one of her dreams that had awakened her. She'd heard Angus's voice again. The sound of the wind had drawn her out onto her balcony and when she'd seen the clouds roll in over the lake, blacking out the stars, she'd known it was time to begin her mission. To right a wrong that she'd done so many years before.

Slipping out of the castle, she'd raced the rain to the stone arch and reached it just as the skies opened. The dreams that had been recurring since her husband's death had centered here in the place that had played such a powerful role in her life and in Angus's.

Her sons and daughters-in-law, who loved her dearly, would not be happy that she regularly sneaked out of the castle in the dead of night. Even less happy that she was

here in the stone arch on a night like this. And she doubted
they would approve of her plan.

So she would make sure that they didn't know.

All her life, she'd been good at keeping secrets. But
since the death of her husband a year ago, one of those
secrets had begun to weigh on her. And the dreams had
begun. Angus was sending them to her. He'd known her
so well, and he'd known that the Stuart sapphires she'd
carried with her to the New World had troubled her con-
science.

Thunder roared and lightning flashed so bright and
fierce that for an instant, Eleanor saw everything clearly—
the garden, the elegant facade of Castle MacPherson, the
cliffs beyond and the roiling waters of the black lake
below.

Home, she thought. Whatever mistakes she may have
made, coming here with Angus Daniel MacPherson fifty
years ago was not one of them. She'd turned her back on
her home in the highlands of Scotland, the pride and expectations of her family, and a man who'd claimed to love
her very much. And she'd never looked back.

Not that Angus had given her any choice.

The memory made her smile and set her mind drift-
ing back to that night in Scotland so long ago, when he'd
asked her to run away with him to the New World. She'd
been shocked at the idea, thrilled and frightened at the
same time. They'd been standing beneath a stone arch in
the gardens of her family's home. Its location in an isolated part of the garden made it a perfect place for them
to meet in secret.

And secrecy was essential. She shouldn't have even
talked to him. Even though their families' lands shared
a common border, the MacPhersons and the Campbells
had been blood enemies for years.

And she'd been promised to another man.

But once Angus had kissed her beneath the stone arch he'd completely captured her heart. Her mother and older sisters had warned her about the legend surrounding the stones. They carried a power from ancient times, and the man you kissed beneath that arch would be your true love forever.

And she hadn't just kissed Angus once. Each time she'd met with him she'd kissed him again and again. And each time she'd promised herself it would be the last time.

The night of Angus's proposal, her family had thrown a ball to formalize her upcoming wedding to her betrothed. She was wearing her future husband's gift to her, the legendary sapphire earrings and necklace that had been bequeathed to his family for service to the Scottish court during the reign of Mary Stuart. The queen had worn them at her coronation, so they were priceless. He'd insisted she wear them tonight as proof of his love for her and as a symbol of the union of their two families.

When she'd slipped away from the ball to meet Angus, she'd planned to say goodbye.

She'd been repeating the little speech to herself all day. She was betrothed to another man, she couldn't go back on her word, and their situation was impossible. There was no way that their families would allow them to marry. In fact, her father would probably inflict bodily harm on Angus.

Eleanor slipped her hand into her pocket and closed her fingers around the leather pouches where she kept the sapphires. The only time she'd worn them was for her wedding portrait that hung in the main parlor of the castle. The jewels always reminded her of the man she'd betrayed and left behind. Everyone had always believed that they were her dowry, and she'd kept silent all of these years.

If only she'd left the necklace and earrings behind with

the man who'd given them to her. At least their families would have had the sapphires. But there'd been no time. Angus, impatient, impetuous, irresistible, hadn't allowed her any. And when she'd initially refused to go with him that night, he hadn't taken no for an answer. He'd simply carried her away.

Thank God.

Her heart tightened as she thought of how he'd completely swept her up in his belief in their future.

Lightning flashed again, illuminating the visual reality of that belief. Angus had promised to build a castle and gardens for her in a setting that would remind her of all that she was leaving behind in Scotland. He'd kept his word. The lovely lakes and mountains in the Adirondack region had kept her from getting too homesick during those early years. He'd kept his promise to build a replica of the stone arch in her family's garden. He'd even brought some stones from the original, and when it was complete she'd stood with him here just as she'd stood with him beneath the one in Scotland.

That was when the legend of Castle MacPherson's stone arch had begun. Over the years she'd lost count of the number of times Angus had told and retold the story of how she'd captivated him, heart and mind, that first time they'd kissed beneath the stone arch in her family's garden. And the story had spread, being told and retold throughout the community. Her children had believed in it and they'd each married their mates right here.

The little pain around her heart increased. In the year since he'd passed she'd missed him so much. But she always sensed his presence when she stood here in the place where they'd laughed and loved and dreamed together so many times.

And the stones had played a part in the dream she was

sure that Angus was sending her. In them, she always saw the same thing. A young woman with reddish curls dropping to her knees at the side of the arch and lifting a leather pouch out of a pile of loose stones. Inside, the young woman always found one of the earrings. Not the pair or the necklace.

Eleanor tightened her fingers around the pouch she held in her pocket. As she did, she heard Angus's voice in her ear, just as clearly as she heard it in her dreams.

"Her name is Adair. She believes in the power of the stones enough to bury her own dreams and fantasies beneath them. You must hide one of the earrings in the stone arch for her to find. When she finds it, the Stuart Sapphires will begin to find their way home. You can finally rest easy. Trust me, Ellie—just as you did on the night we ran away."

The rain had stopped, and a few stars had reappeared in the sky. With Angus's words still in her mind, Eleanor stepped out of the arch and began to work some of the stones loose. And when the earring was safely buried and she returned to the castle, she slept peacefully.

1

AN AFFAIR TO remember.

That had been the guarantee that Adair MacPherson had given to Rexie Maitland and her parents when they'd signed the contract to hold their daughter's wedding and reception at Castle MacPherson.

And she intended to deliver. She had to. There were already two big *X* marks in the failure column of her life. She didn't need a third one.

Adair pressed a firm hand to the nerves jittering in her stomach. The first step on her way to her goal, the wedding rehearsal scheduled for today, had gotten off to a rocky start. The high-strung bride had gone into a panic attack when the groom-to-be hadn't arrived on time. But Adair's aunt and business partner, Viola MacPherson, had warded off a full meltdown with a cup of herb tea. And the tardy Lawrence Banes, a suave, sort of George Clooney look-alike with a good fifteen years on the bride, had finally arrived, full of apologies.

Pulling off the Maitland/Banes wedding on Saturday

was crucial to the launch of her new business plan, one that would establish the reputation of Castle MacPherson as a premier wedding destination in the heart of New York's Adirondacks. Adair swept her gaze around the garden.

The setting was perfect. The gray stone castle she and her sisters had grown up in stood on a rocky promontory at the far eastern end of Glen Loch Lake. Three stories high and rectangular in shape, it sat tucked between two mountains, boasted spectacular views, and its gardens, thanks to her Aunt Vi, had graced the pages of several gardening magazines.

The Maitland/Banes wedding would take place beneath the stone arch her several-times-great-grandfather Angus One had built for the stolen bride he'd brought here from Scotland. Now the tardy Mr. Banes was standing beneath it flanked by the minister and his best man. The maid of honor and the flower girl had lined up just behind the arbor that marked the entrance to the gardens. The mother of the bride, Bunny Maitland, had taken her seat in the first row of chairs, and just in front of the stone arch, Aunt Vi sat, her bow poised over her cello, ready to play on signal.

Everything was perfect, except that the bride-to-be was holding Adair's hand in a death grip.

"I don't know if I can do this," Rexie whispered.

Ignoring her plummeting stomach, Adair took a deep breath and spoke in her calmest voice. "This is only a rehearsal. You have to save those nerves for Saturday."

"I know." Rexie, a pretty twenty-two-year-old blonde and heir to the Maitland fortune, smiled tremulously. "I can't seem to help it. I need to know that I'm doing the right thing. I have to know that the legend will work."

"It will." The power of the legend and the stones was

the one thing in her life that she still had absolute faith in. She might be a bit shaky on her ability to keep this wedding on track, but she had no doubt that the stone arch her ancestor Angus One had built for Eleanor Campbell MacPherson had the power to bring true loves together.

This was the young woman's second go at matrimony. A little over a year ago, her first husband had left her to return to his family's horse farm in Montana. Then Rexie had met Lawrence and six months ago, after reading an article on the history of the MacPhersons and the legend in the *New York Times,* she'd contacted Viola to ask about scheduling her ceremony and reception at the castle because she wanted a guarantee of success this time around.

The *Times* article had created quite a buzz because it had dug up all the rumors that had circulated over the years about the missing sapphires that Eleanor MacPherson had worn in her wedding portrait. The writer had even reprinted an image of Mary Stuart wearing a similar necklace and earrings at her coronation and posed the theory that Eleanor's dowry of jewels had been given to her by the Queen of Scots.

Adair could have kissed the *Times* writer for stirring everything up and giving her the idea for a new business plan.

She took Rexie's other hand in hers. "You are not going to fail this time."

That was the mantra Adair recited to herself each morning. Not that she'd ever failed at marriage—she hadn't had the chance. Six months ago she'd come home to Aunt Vi and the castle to lick her wounds, and they were still fresh. The five-year plan she'd so carefully crafted when she'd finished her MBA had gone south. One day she'd been on the fast track, and the next, the company she'd worked for had downsized and derailed her. Her pink slip had been quickly followed by an email from her boyfriend, Baxter DuBois, terminating their personal relationship, as well.

That's when she'd moved back to the castle. Now with her aunt's help and the power of Angus One's stone arch, she was determined to turn her family home into *the* wedding destination spot in upstate New York.

And the success of Rexie's wedding was key. Mr. and Mrs. Winston Maitland III resided on Long Island but also owned homes in Boca Raton, Florida, and Vail, Colorado. They had the kind of social contacts that could make the reputation of Castle MacPherson.

Or break it.

"I've seen proof of the stones' power in my own father's life," Adair said. "He's kissed two women beneath the stone arch, and if he were here, he'd tell you it was the stones that gave him two chances of finding his true loves. He considers himself a very fortunate man."

Adair held back a little on the details. Her father had taken the loss of her mother so hard that even after he fell in love with Professor Beth Sutherland, it had been a dozen years before he married her. But seven years ago she and her sisters, along with Beth's three triplet sons, had stood beneath the arch while her father, A.D., and Beth had exchanged vows.

"And your father's happy?" Rexie asked.

"Yes. There's real power in the stones. When we were growing up, my sisters and I believed in it so much that we used to write down our dreams and goals and bury them in a metal box beneath some of the loose stones. It was my mother's old jewelry box so it had three different compartments and we all used different colors of paper."

She'd nearly forgotten about that box, Adair realized. On the night of her father's wedding, she'd even written down a particularly erotic fantasy involving Cam Sutherland and buried that, too. She hadn't thought of it in years. And she hadn't seen Cam or his brothers since the wedding. They'd been finishing college that year and each had been focused on career plans that kept them very busy. Last she'd heard, Cam was working overseas for the CIA. For an instant his image flashed brightly into her mind and she could see him just as he'd looked that day—the dark, unruly hair, the blue eyes that had always held a dare.

And Cam Sutherland was the last thing she needed to be thinking about right now. If she didn't get this wedding rehearsal on track, an "affair to remember" was going to take on a whole new, horrible meaning.

She focused on the hint of panic in Rexie's eyes. And a solution suddenly occurred to her. "Look, why don't we tap into the power of the legend right now?"

"How?"

"This is just a rehearsal and you won't actually say your vows, but why don't you kiss Lawrence? If you do that today while you're beneath the stone arch, then you should be all set. In the legend, it's the kiss that does the trick."

"Really?" Rexie shifted her gaze to where her groom-to-be waited. He was on his cell phone.

"It's guaranteed," Adair assured her. "Why don't we start? Everyone is in place."

"Except for my father," Rexie said, her lip trembling. "He's taking another call on his cell."

"Mr. Maitland?" Adair spoke in a low tone, but she kept Rexie's hand firmly gripped in hers.

The bride-to-be's father held up one finger, but he never stopped talking into his phone. Winston Maitland, a tall stocky man with thinning gray hair, had pretty much had his cell glued to his ear since he'd arrived. So had the groom-to-be for that matter. The jerks. Adair wanted to shake both of them.

That was when she heard it. Just the whisper of thunder. Damn. Keeping Rexie's hand in a death grip, she angled her head just enough to catch sight of a cluster of dark clouds at the far end of the lake.

A quick glance around told her that so far she was the only one who'd noticed. The sky overhead was bright blue, the garden bathed in sunlight. She sent up a quick prayer that the storm would stay put.

Alba, the white whippet mix her aunt Vi had recently brought home from a shelter, rose from where she'd plopped herself a few feet away on a patch of sun-drenched grass. She shot a look out over the lake, and whined. Adair followed the direction of the dog's gaze and so did Rexie. The clouds were rolling closer.

"Look. It's going to rain," Rexie said. "That's not a good sign. Maybe we should postpone this."

Adair tightened her grip on Rexie's hand. "No. It's still quite a ways off. We just have to get started."

Alba whined again, then made a beeline in the direction of the castle, the bell around her neck emphasizing her departure.

Not a good sign.

Though Alba was deaf, her other senses were spot-on, and Adair was willing to bet she could sense the approaching storm. So could the mother of the bride, Bunny Maitland, who sent her a worried look.

Adair tried for a serene smile. The clouds were still a good distance away, she assured herself. Time enough to panic once the lightning started. She waved to get her aunt's attention.

Viola MacPherson had moved to the castle after Adair's mom, Marianne, had died. She'd been four, her sisters three and one. Their father had buried himself in his painting, so it was their aunt who'd raised them. She'd given

up her job at the nearby college and devoted her life to
creating a home for them while providing a haven where
their father could continue with his landscape painting.

Now in her late fifties, Viola looked and projected the
energy of a much younger woman. Adair had inherited her
aunt's tiny stature as well as the curse of naturally curly
red hair. Viola's cascade of ringlets was gray now, and
she managed them by pulling them back from her face.
She favored long skirts or wide-leg pants and tunics that
went with her gypsy look.

At a signal from Adair, Vi began to play Beethoven's
"Ode to Joy."

Thunder sounded faintly in the distance.

Refusing to look out over the lake again, Adair directed
the flower girl to start down the short path that led from
the rose garden to the stone arch. When the little girl was
halfway there, Adair gestured to the maid of honor.

"Daddy's still on his phone," Rexie whispered.

"Mr. Maitland." Adair spoke in a low tone.

Frowning at Adair, the man stuffed his cell in a pocket
and moved to his daughter's side. "That was an important call."

Adair smiled at him. "And this is a very important moment for your daughter. Go."

Thunder rumbled—closer this time.

Rexie and her father were halfway to the minister when
the dark clouds settled like a lid over the garden with
such speed and finality she wondered they hadn't heard
a loud clang.

Lightning flashed behind her just as Rexie and her
dad made it to the shelter of the stone arch. Adair hurried
up the path, grabbing Bunny's arm on the way. Together
they power-walked to join the rest of the wedding party.

Cello in hand, Aunt Vi was the last to make it before

the next crack of thunder sounded. Then for a moment, no one spoke as they huddled shoulder to shoulder and watched nature put on a powerful show. Lightning criss-crossed the sky at times so bright Adair found herself blinking. The intermittent explosions of thunder made her wonder if this was what it might be like to be trapped in a bunker during an attack.

And her mind flashed back to the night of her father's wedding. There'd been a storm like this that night, also. The Sutherland boys, Reid, Cam and Duncan, had flown in just for the wedding and then gone back to their colleges right after the ceremony. She and her sisters hadn't seen them since that long-ago summer when the boys' mother, Beth, had been a visiting professor at nearby Huntleigh College and she'd gotten her father's permission to use the library at the castle for the research she was doing for a historical novel she was writing on the MacPherson clan.

That was the summer when Adair's fascination with Cam had begun. Because she'd hated him. He'd been a relentless tease, always pulling her curls and calling her "Princess" because she lived in a "castle." And he'd constantly nagged her to try things she'd never tried before—like climbing over the stone arch.

There were days during that summer when she'd wanted to strangle him.

But strangling hadn't been on her mind the night of her father's wedding to Beth Sutherland. Because in the twelve years that had passed, the Sutherlands had changed. Drastically. From annoying, know-it-all ten-year-olds to attractive young men.

What hadn't changed had been her fascination with Cam. It had flared immediately from the instant he'd arrived at the castle that day.

They weren't kids on a playdate any more. And while

their parents had been pledging their vows beneath the stone arch, her eyes had locked on his, and she'd wanted him in a way that she'd never wanted anyone—or anything. It had thrilled her, terrified her. And it had fueled the fantasy that she'd committed to paper and put into the special metal box that she and her sisters had hidden away in the stone arch.

Lightning flashed again and the thunder roared, instantaneous and deafening, refocusing her thoughts on the present.

Vi whispered in her ear. "This isn't good."

Adair had to agree with her aunt. In all her years growing up at the castle, she'd never seen a storm like this one. And it had to happen the day of Rexie Maitland's wedding rehearsal.

They were so tightly packed in the space that Adair had to crane her neck to meet Rexie's eyes. Panic was what she saw and she felt an answering surge in herself. Pushing it down, she kept her voice calm and spaced her words to fit in between the claps of thunder. "We should go forward with the rehearsal."

Not sure how much Rexie heard in the cacophony of sound bombarding them, Adair pursed her lips and pantomimed a kiss. Then she held her breath, willing Rexie to kiss Lawrence and seal the deal. Not for the first time, she wished she had at least a smidgen of the power Macbeth's witches had.

Thunder cracked so loud Adair was certain the rocks beneath her feet moved. Aunt Vi grabbed her hand and held on hard. Adair kept her gaze on Rexie, her willpower on at full throttle.

Finally, Rexie turned to Lawrence and put her hands on his shoulders to get his attention. A second later, he began to lower his head.

Lightning flashed, so close this time that Adair could smell it, and the ground beneath them shook—enough to tear Rexie out of Lawrence's arms just before their lips met and thrust her backward into the minister. Adair heard stones tumble from the front of the arch before thunder deafened her.

When the earth stilled again, Adair found herself held tightly in her aunt Vi's arms, a cello pressed hard against her thigh. Rexie was in her mother's arms. Not good. Lawrence and Winston had their heads close. The maid of honor had picked up the flower girl and the best man had slumped onto a ledge, his face sheet-white.

When the storm had moved off so that conversation was a possibility, everyone began to talk at once, their voices pitched almost as low as the now-fading thunder. But the main consensus was that the stone arch they were standing under had just been struck by lightning.

Vi was looking at the stones that formed the arch over their heads. "We're lucky they held, but we should have someone check them."

Adair figured checking the stone arch was the least of her problems. The biggest one was headed toward her, elbowing her way through the group. When Rexie reached her, she said, "I'm calling off the wedding." Then she burst into tears.

2

An hour later, Adair stepped out of her room and went in search of her aunt. After finally seeing the Maitlands off, she'd spent some time in the shower replaying everything that had happened in her mind, going over the should-have-saids and could-have-dones. Her ex-boyfriend Bax had always criticized her for trying to second-guess herself.

Maybe he'd been right. In the downsizing at her former company, he'd kept his job. She hadn't.

Pushing that thought out of her mind, she went back to her replay. The shouting match that had occurred after the lightning strike and Rexie's hysterical announcement had rivaled the storm for intensity. Mr. Maitland had claimed the lightning strike was a sign they should change the venue for the ceremony back to Long Island, which had triggered a fresh eruption of tears from the bride and a yelling match between her parents. Using the noise as a cover, she'd told the groom that he'd better soothe his bride-to-be.

The fact that she'd had to jump-start him had bothered her. If he hadn't been late for the rehearsal, the storm and the lightning strike wouldn't have been an issue. But he'd said something to Rexie that had calmed her while she concentrated on the parents.

Before they'd driven away, Rexie had agreed to postpone her decision to cancel the wedding. The men had departed for Long Island but Adair had booked Rexie and Bunny into the Eagle's Nest, a bed-and-breakfast in the nearby village of Glen Loch, so they could return to the castle in the morning when their nerves had settled to give her their decision. The one thing that Rexie had remained firm on was that if the wedding was going forward, it would be held at Castle MacPherson.

Which was exactly what she wanted, too. Wasn't it?

And why was that even a question she was thinking about? Of course she wanted the wedding to go forward. What kind of a businesswoman was she? Good ones didn't sabotage their own business plans.

She just had to keep her focus. But it was hard to ignore that lightning strike, or the fact that it had occurred at the exact moment when Lawrence was about to kiss Rexie and seal the deal.

The moment she stepped out onto the veranda that ran along the back of the house and spotted Vi sitting at a table with an opened bottle of wine and two glasses, some of her tension eased. It didn't surprise her that her aunt had chosen this place to wait for her. The back of the castle, with its flagstone terraces dropping in levels to the lake, had always been one of Adair's favorite spots. She noted that the water was calm and stunningly blue, its surface a perfect reflection of the now-cloudless sky overhead. The only reminder of the violent storm was a fading rainbow.

Alba lay sprawled nearby on the flagstones, totally exhausted by the day. Adair could certainly sympathize with the feeling, but her own day had a ways to go. There was a decision to be made.

She joined her aunt and accepted the glass of wine.

Vi clinked her glass to Adair's. "To a job well done."

"I haven't done anything yet."

Vi sampled the wine. "You've weathered a lightning strike, you've calmed down a very upset bride and her parents. And you'll see to it that more rational minds will prevail in the morning."

"And what if I'm wrong?"

"Wrong in what way?"

Setting her wine down, Adair reached out and took one of her aunt's hands. "You know how much I want this wedding to take place on Saturday."

Vi brought her other hand to cover her niece's in a gesture that was achingly familiar to Adair.

"Ever since you were a child, whenever you've set yourself a goal you've achieved it. Not only that, you egged your younger sisters into setting their own goals. Look where they are right now. Piper is working for a famous defense attorney in D.C., and Nell is touring the country on a grant that allows her to teach creative writing classes in disadvantaged schools and at the same time, promote her first children's story."

Adair shook her head. "I'm not doing that well in the goal achievement game anymore."

"Why on earth would you think that?"

"Because the first curveball that life threw at me…" She paused and waved her free hand. "I ran away and came back here. I'm not proud of that."

Vi studied her for a moment. "You're not your father, Adair. If that's what you're worried about."

Perhaps it was, Adair thought. Her aunt had always been able to hit the nail on the head. Perhaps that fear was at the heart of the gnawing anxiety she'd felt ever since she'd left Chicago.

"When your mother, Marianne, died, he did run," Vi said. "He hid for years, burying himself in his art and his teaching at the college."

"I've never understood him. He met Beth Sutherland when I was nine, the summer that she did her research in the library and we had all those long afternoon playdates with the Sutherland boys. Nell saw Dad kiss her once beneath the stones. We thought they might get married and that we'd all become a family. But then she went back to Chicago and he went back to his painting and we didn't see any of them again until the wedding seven years ago. And Beth and Dad are so happy now, traveling the world, each pursuing their dreams. Why did they wait?"

"Because they needed to. They had young children to think about, careers to pursue. She came here to do her research shortly after her husband had been found guilty of fraud and sent to prison. His family was wealthy and they tried to sue for custody. She felt that building her career was essential to holding on to her sons. And your father always had his art to return to. They waited for a better time. That's where you're different, Adair. You don't wait for anything."

Adair blinked. "I don't?"

Vi laughed. "Good Lord, I can barely keep up with you. You didn't even have your bags all unpacked when that feature writer from the *Times* visited us for an interview. I could almost see the lightbulb go on over your head. The very next day you were plotting out a business plan for the castle. And when the article stirred up interest in the legend and Eleanor's missing sapphires, you had brochures printed to hand out to the tourists who started arriving on the weekends."

Adair shrugged. "I just capitalized on the buzz the rumors of a missing and possibly priceless collection of gems created. They'll die down again."

"The point I'm making is that you didn't hesitate to capitalize on that buzz to promote the legend surrounding the stones. I've never known you to hide, Adair. And while you were showering and changing, I'm betting you marshaled together a strategy for handling Bunny and Rexie tomorrow morning."

Adair took a sip of her wine. "I think I've got that covered. Sure, lightning struck during the rehearsal, but did it do any permanent damage? No. The stone arch is still there. Indestructible. So it still has the power to unite Rexie with the love of her life on Saturday. And that marriage will be just as indestructible."

"Very nice argument."

"Yeah. If Lawrence Banes *is* the love of her life," Adair said. "He was late to the rehearsal, and it was his schedule that had required it to take place two days before the wedding. Plus, he was texting on his cell instead of trying to support Rexie when she became hysterical after the lightning strike."

Vi merely met her eyes, saying nothing. It was a ploy that her aunt had used very successfully when she and her sisters had been trying to explain some of the mischief they'd gotten into.

"Okay, maybe he's just a jerk," she conceded. "A jerk she's in love with."

"Or maybe he's just as nervous as the bride. When you first explained your business plan to me you defined our role pretty clearly."

Adair raised a hand, palm out. "Right. We're not matchmakers or relationship counselors. Our job is to provide the perfect wedding and let the stone arch do its work."

She rose then and walked to the low stone wall that

bordered the veranda. Beyond the gardens she could see the curve of the stone arch. Vi joined her and put an arm around her shoulder. "But? I hear a *but* in there."

"I can't help thinking that's what the lightning strike was about. I suggested to Rexie that she kiss Lawrence today during the rehearsal to seal the deal. That way she could walk down the aisle on Saturday knowing that she was marrying her true love. But the lightning prevented the kiss. Maybe the power of the stones is working against this wedding."

Even as she said the words, an image from an old movie filled her mind—a bride running down the aisle. Quickly, she shoved it aside. That kind of thing didn't happen in real life. Did it? "We really need to pull off this wedding, Aunt Vi."

Vi gave her a hug. "Then you're going to find a way to do it. Why don't you go down to the arch now and think about it while I get started on dinner. Use the power."

Shoving her hands in her pockets, Adair moved around the veranda's low wall and started down one of the paths. Gardening wasn't her thing. She couldn't even begin to name the plants that bloomed everywhere in profusion.

Except for the roses. And she'd recognized the lilacs and violets earlier in the spring. Gardening was one of her aunt Vi's talents. Angus One had built the original garden for Eleanor but it had been well tended by their descendants. In fact, all the MacPhersons who'd been born and raised here at the castle had benefitted from a very rich gene pool. Some of them had turned to education. It was one of her great-great-uncles who'd been a cofounder of the nearby Huntleigh College. There were three paintings in the castle that bore Eleanor's signature. And Angus One was credited with the design of the castle. And he had to have had some serious engineering skills to have pulled off the construction of the stone arch.

Stepping out of the gardens, she crossed the grass verge until she reached the row of chairs they'd placed in front of the stones for the rehearsal. The arch itself was ten feet tall at its center, ten feet long and eight feet wide. The summer the Sutherland triplets had played here, they'd measured it off to the inch.

The boys had been ten that year, she'd been nine and her sisters eight and six. They'd been fascinated by the Sutherlands. Cam in particular had intrigued her. They'd taken turns deciding the games they would play on those long afternoons. And the ones Cam chose had been her favorites. There was always a risk involved, something that made her heart race faster.

His favorite game had been "pirate and treasure." More than once he'd chosen her as his partner, and together they'd climbed up the cliff face to the west of the castle. Adair's heart raced just thinking about it. Aunt Vi and her father had always forbidden them to go to the cliffs. But they could hardly admit that to the Sutherlands.

When she realized she was smiling, Adair made herself stop. She hadn't come here to the stone arch to think about Cam Sutherland. She'd managed not to think about him for years. She hadn't even seen him since that night after their parents' wedding, when she and her sisters had come out here with a bottle of champagne to write out their secret fantasies about their ideal fantasy lovers.

She'd written her fantasy about Cam. She hadn't been able to get him out of her head from the instant her eyes had met his during the ceremony. In that moment of eye contact only, no one else had existed. The intensity of the awareness she'd felt, the depth of it, had been something she'd never experienced before. When he'd asked her to dance later, she'd seen the challenge in his eyes. He'd known the effect he was having on her. But she'd refused the dance, preferring the safety she'd felt in his brother Reid's arms.

It was only later, with a little help from the champagne, that she'd given full flight to her desire and her fantasy. Just thinking about it made her knees feel so weak that she sank onto the narrow ledge that ran along the side of the arch. Cam spelled trouble for her. And she didn't kid herself. She'd increased the problem exponentially when she'd written her fantasy down on paper and buried it in the arch.

The whole thing had been her idea, and she'd talked her sisters into doing the same thing. Adair the great planner. In the back of her mind she'd had some idea that if she wrote a fantasy about Reid or Duncan, she could negate what she was feeling for Cam.

Hadn't worked out. The instant her pen had struck paper, it had all been about Cam and no one but Cam.

Calm down. Adair forced herself to breathe in, breathe out.

You've avoided him for years. His job at the CIA has kept him overseas. There's nothing to worry about.

Except the power of the stones.

And there might be a way to lessen that....

Dropping to her knees, Adair traced her fingers along the base of the arch, trying to find the loose stones that she and her sisters had discovered when they were children. Behind them there was a niche just big enough to hold the metal box they'd used for years. Any fantasy that she'd put into the box could be taken out. Then she just might have less to worry about.

None of the stones were loose.

That couldn't be. Lowering herself to her stomach,

Adair squinted at the stones as she ran her hands along them again. There wasn't even a crack she could get a finger into.

Had the lightning shifted things?

The sound of Alba's bell had her scrambling to her feet. Once the dog reached the arch, she wandered around to the side and started pawing at some stones. Adair spotted her aunt as she stepped out of the gardens.

"Find any damage?" Vi called.

"Seems pretty solid." Adair brushed her hands off on her slacks. And she was going to put that box and the fantasies it contained out of her mind. Why on earth was she obsessing about Cam Sutherland all of a sudden? Avoidance had worked so far, and there wasn't any reason to think that it wouldn't continue to work.

Unless you don't want it to....

Pushing the thought firmly away, Adair stepped out of the stone arch. "I have an idea about how to avoid the runaway bride disaster."

Vi smiled at her. "I'm all ears."

"You distract Bunny tomorrow and give me some time alone with Rexie. Maybe she'll tell me what's bothering her. I'd like to know what really happened with her first husband that's making her so nervous about taking a second chance."

Vi smiled. "I can handle Bunny. She's very interested in getting the recipe for the scones I served with her herb tea."

"You never give that recipe out."

"I won't this time either, but I have several older versions of it that I can bear to part with."

Alba's bell jingled again, and she suddenly appeared around the side of the arch with something in her mouth.

The dog dropped what looked like a leather pouch on the ground at their feet.

She and Vi dropped to their knees together. Then Adair picked up the pouch. It was folded like an envelope with another pouch inside of it and another pouch in side of that. "Chinese boxes," Adair murmured.

But when she opened the last one, all she could do was stare. Inside lay a sapphire earring set in gold. The gem was the size of her thumbnail and it dangled from a link of gold chain.

Vi caught her breath. "Oh, my."

Oh, my, indeed. Adair recognized it right away. Eleanor Campbell MacPherson was wearing it in the portrait that hung in the main parlor. And Mary Stuart might very well have worn it on the day she was crowned.

But Eleanor's dowry had been missing for years. The theory was that one of the Anguses had sold it long ago.

With the earring still lying in the palm of her hand, she stood and walked around to the side of the stone arch where Alba had been digging. Sure enough, there was a pile of stones that looked as if they'd shaken loose during the storm.

"Who on earth put this here and why?" Adair breathed.

Alba began to bark. When Adair glanced at her, she saw that the dog wasn't looking at the loose stones but at the wooded hill that sloped sharply upward beyond the stone arch. Alba continued to bark as she raced to the hedge that separated the gardens from the trees. Adair ran her gaze up the hill, trying to see what was upsetting the dog, but she saw nothing.

"There's something up there she doesn't like," Vi said as she moved past Adair to take the dog's collar and pat her head.

Even as the dog quieted, Adair scanned the hill again and still saw nothing.

"We'd better get that earring inside and then we'll have to call your father and let him know," Vi said.

Adair stared down at the earring and as she did, it seemed to glow. She could have sworn that she felt a warmth in her hands. After all these years, a part of Eleanor's dowry had shown up. Why now, she couldn't help but wonder. And why had it been hidden away in the stone arch?

3

Received a call from Mom and A.D. Need our help. Conference call with all three of us at five-thirty?

CAM SUTHERLAND READ the short text from his brother Reid twice. Some things never changed. In spite of the fact that he and his brothers were triplets, there'd always been a pecking order. From the time they were little, if his mom needed something she'd always called on Reid, the oldest. Even now, she used him as her main contact person, and it was his job to relay the information and/or request.

Because his younger brother Duncan had always been studious and a bit shy, he'd always seemed to receive extra attention, too. Not that his mom had a lot to spread around. Her work teaching and her research had always absorbed her. "Absentminded professor" might have been a term coined to describe her. But after their father had been sent to prison, Beth Sutherland's academic success and her publications had been key to keeping custody of her sons. So from the age of ten, they'd all pitched in.

And they'd fallen into roles. Reid had become the leader and organizer, Duncan had offered ideas and analysis, and it had usually fallen on Cam to carry out the missions. Not that he'd complained. He'd always preferred action over giving advice or orders.

His mother didn't turn to them very often anymore, but he had no doubt that he would probably get the assignment. His older brother's new duties in the Secret Service serving on the Vice President's security detail were keeping Reid very busy, and the last time he'd talked to Duncan, who worked as a profiler in the Behavioral Sciences division of the FBI, he'd been consulting on a case in Montana.

Then with a frown Cam read the text again. His mom and A. D. MacPherson were in Scotland, and if they'd taken the time to call, his best guess was that something was going on at the castle. From what he'd last heard, Viola MacPherson lived alone there now. The image of a tiny, energetic woman popped into his mind. He hadn't forgotten her scones or her brownies. Except for Christmas and birthday cards, he hadn't seen Aunt Vi or visited the castle since his mother had married the successful landscape painter seven years ago. That had been his senior year in college and he'd joined the CIA right away. For five years he'd worked a variety of covert operations overseas. He'd enjoyed the travel and the challenge of the assignments, but when an opportunity had presented itself to transfer to the Domestic Operations section in D.C., he'd been ready for a change. He still worked in the field but his assignments tended to be of shorter duration, and as a side benefit he got to work for an old and dear friend.

The last he'd heard, the MacPherson sisters had been as busy as he, his brothers and their parents, and were pursuing career goals. Not that he knew what they were doing exactly. He'd avoided thinking about them for years.

Especially Adair.

He strode to the window of his office, but it wasn't

the scenery that he saw. It was Adair MacPherson's face. The image of her standing beneath that stone arch during his mother's wedding to A. D. MacPherson had been popping into his mind lately. It had been a late-fall wedding. He and his brothers had been tied up in classes so they'd booked flights that arrived on the morning of the ceremony and left that evening.

The picture he'd carried in his mind before that had been of a little girl with red curls and freckles, a face that had frowned easily when he'd teased her, and a temper that he'd enjoyed igniting. Calling her "Princess" usually succeeded in eliciting both responses. But she had a smile that he'd wanted to trigger almost as much as the frown.

What he'd enjoyed most about her during those long summer afternoons when they'd played together was the fact that she was willing to try anything. Eager, in fact. She'd been fun—for a girl.

But what he'd felt at his mother's wedding had been something else. And that was the image that still lingered in his mind. Her red-gold curls were tied back with a green ribbon. He'd wanted to run his hands through those curls. At nine, her body had been sturdy and athletic. At twenty, it had been slim as a wand, and he'd wanted to explore every single inch of it. Desire was far too tame a word for what he'd felt. But it was her eyes that had nearly finished him off that day. He had no clear idea of how long he had looked into them. But he'd never forget the color— a pale and misty green that he could have sworn he was drowning in.

Cam drew in a deep breath and let it out. He'd wanted her that day in a way he'd never wanted anyone or anything before. In a way he'd never wanted anyone since. And he'd been rash enough to ask her to dance. If she'd agreed, if he'd held her in his arms, he still wasn't sure what would have happened. Perhaps she'd had some idea of the possible consequences because she'd turned him down flat.

He wasn't sure why she was popping into his mind more frequently lately. Perhaps because he was back in the States. Perhaps because she'd never really left his mind. Perhaps because it was only possible to avoid something for so long and then...

"Got a minute, Sutherland?"

Cam turned as his boss walked into the room. Seven years ago Daryl Garnett had recruited him to work for the CIA. Cam had trained under the man at the farm and Daryl had been one of his mentors ever since, and he'd invited Cam to join the Domestic Operations section he headed up in D.C.

"I think I just got something on my old nemesis." Daryl moved around Cam's desk and taped two photos on the whiteboard that covered nearly one wall. "Meet Gianni Scalzo."

Cam turned to study the photos. He'd seen one of them before because Daryl carried a smaller version in his wallet, the way a man might carry a photo of his family. But Gianni Scalzo wasn't family. He was a con man extraordinaire who'd put a bullet in Daryl's knee and limited his career as a covert field operative.

Since then, Daryl had been steadily working his way up in the training and management side of the Agency, but he'd made a hobby out of tracking Scalzo down.

In the photo that Cam had seen before, Scalzo had long, curly, shoulder-length hair—Mel Gibson in the first *Lethal Weapon*. In shorts and sunglasses, he looked very much at home on the prow of a sailboat. The man standing next to him in the picture was shorter, less athletic in build, the kind of man that you wouldn't notice if you passed him on the street. Interpol believed he was Scalzo's partner. Daryl agreed. Both men were masters at disguise, but the partner had always stayed in the shadows.

The man in the second photo was older. His short dark hair boasted just a sprinkle of gray and he had a well-trimmed mustache and goatee. Not Mel Gibson but he still had a sort of middle-aged movie star quality. Next to him stood a pretty young blonde.

"What do you think?" Daryl asked.

"It's a difficult call. The more important question is what do you think? You're the one who met him in person."

"Allowing for the passage of time, I'm betting they're one and the same," Daryl said. "I felt it as soon as I saw the picture. I had one of our techs run a facial analysis of the two photos."

Cam moved closer to study the two images more closely. "What were the results?"

"Inconclusive." A tall lanky man in his mid-fifties, Daryl stood shoulder to shoulder with Cam at the whiteboard. "Right now, I'm having someone age the photo of Scalzo on the sailboat."

"How long have you been looking for Scalzo now?" Cam asked.

Daryl tapped the leg that had retired him from the field. "Fifteen years, three months and nine days."

"The age difference is about right. Who tipped you off to take a look at the guy?" Cam asked.

"Ben Slack contacted me an hour ago and I asked him to email me the photo," Daryl said. "He was in your class at the farm."

Cam remembered Ben, and anyone who had been trained by Daryl would know of his interest in tracking Scalzo down.

"Ben says the Securities and Exchange Commission is 'looking at' this guy," Daryl said. "One problem I've always had in tracing Scalzo was that the man avoids getting his picture taken. But this guy is getting married, so he couldn't very well refuse to have an engagement picture published."

"What else have you got?" Cam asked.

"If the Securities and Exchange Commission is sniffing around him, he could be using the same M.O. as Scalzo did in Italy, and the same one that he used in Portland a few years ago. I was nearly in time to get him. He changes looks, identities and locations, but the scam he and his partner run remains the same. They target financial planners—some who handle select clients as well as others who manage pension funds. Scalzo is always the front man. He infiltrates the social strata first—buys an estate, joins the right clubs. That's exactly what this guy has been doing in the Long Island area for the last year and a half. He promises huge returns to his investors and he delivers them. After the recent scandals, that's enough to bring him to the attention of the Securities and Exchange Commission."

"It sounds like the same kind of scam my father tried to run, but your nemesis is much better at it."

Daryl's hand settled on Cam's shoulder. He didn't have to say a word. As the man who'd recruited Cam, Daryl had accessed all the details on his father's background. A rich and pampered young man, Cam's dad, David Fedderman, had relied on his parents to buy him out of scrapes all of his life. Once he'd joined Fedderman Trust, he'd spent all of his time wining and dining clients and traveling to locate new investment opportunities. When it had finally been revealed that he'd been dipping into clients' accounts to the tune of hundreds of thousands, his parents hadn't been able to buy Davie out of serving jail time. They had, however, tried to get custody of Cam and his brothers in a brutal lawsuit. But Beth's lawyer had finally prevailed and she'd immediately changed their last name to hers—Sutherland. They hadn't heard from any of the Feddermans since.

What wasn't in all the files was the fact that his father hadn't been any more skilled at being a father or a husband than he'd been at being a crook. Cam had been ten when it had all gone down, and what he recalled most was that after the arrest, he'd never heard his mother cry herself to sleep anymore.

Daryl looked at him then. "Any chance you could help me out with this?"

Cam smiled at him. "I thought you'd never ask. Do we have any way to connect this guy to the Portland crime?"

"That's what I'll start on next. Scalzo's good." His smile widened. "But the Portland police have a set of prints for the alias he operated under there. I've got a call into the P.D. there right now."

Cam tapped the second man in the sailboat photo. "What about his partner?"

"There's no sign of him. He stays out of sight, out of mind."

"What's your plan?"

"I've got some vacation time coming, so I'm going to take a few days to see what I can dig up on Long Island," Daryl said. "Maybe I can get a whiff of the partner or a glimpse of Scalzo. I think I can recognize him in person."

"Let me know what you need on this end." Then he remembered Reid's text. "But I may have to make a quick trip up to the Adirondacks to check out a family thing."

Daryl grinned at him. "Luck is on my side." He pointed to the engagement photo of the man he was sure was

Scalzo. "My friend here is getting married in this little place in the Adirondacks this coming Saturday. Castle MacPherson. Ever heard of it?"

Cam stared at him. "Yeah. As a matter of fact, I have. That's my stepfather's place."

"So you're familiar with it?"

"Somewhat." Not enough to know that people were scheduling weddings there. He turned to his desk, did a quick search for Castle MacPherson on his computer and found himself looking at Adair's smiling face. The impact of just seeing her stopped him short for a minute. The fancy wedding hairdo was gone. But the eyes were the same pale, mysterious green. He had to remind himself to take a breath.

"A wedding destination spot, huh?"

Realizing that Daryl was leaning over his shoulder reading the computer screen, Cam reined in his thoughts and scanned the web page. By the time he finished, he'd noted Vi's photo also, along with a shot of the castle, the gardens and the stone arch. And he'd clicked on a link that led to a small feature article in the *New York Times* that provided a brief history of the castle as well as the story of the legend and Eleanor Campbell MacPherson's missing sapphires.

"And here I thought that wedding destinations involved sandy beaches and drinks with little umbrellas in them," Daryl remarked. "But I guess a stone arch with the promise of a happy-ever-after would have a definite draw. Do you know if the two women are alone up there?"

"They won't be for long." Turning, he glanced back up at the photos on his whiteboard. "I'm going to be an unofficial guest at the upcoming wedding."

"Thanks." Daryl patted him on the shoulder. "I'll need

a day to get my ducks all in a row and make sure he's my guy. Then I'll get in touch."

BY THE TIME five-thirty rolled around, Cam had his own ducks lined up and he was ready to hit the road for the castle. He answered Reid's call on the first ring and once he and his brothers had exchanged greetings, he said, "Problem solved. I'm about to give Vi a call to let her know that I'll be leaving later tonight." Suiting the action to words, he stepped into the elevator and pushed the button to the garage.

"How did you know Mom and A.D. wanted one of us to go up there?" Reid asked.

"I called her," Cam said. "You sent me the text an hour ago. Just because you're the oldest and Mom always calls you doesn't mean Duncan or I can't take the initiative."

"You tell him, bro," Duncan said, laughing.

"I thought we should discuss it first. What if we all took the initiative and we'd all dropped everything to run up there?" Reid asked with just a trace of annoyance in his tone.

"I checked," Cam explained. "Duncan's in Montana and you're on the way to Dulles right now because the Vice President is flying to Paris."

"How did you—?" Reid began.

"He's CIA," Duncan said. "And, as the middle brother, he always has to show off."

"And I'm usually the one who gets the field assignments," Cam pointed out. "I figured I'd get started."

"Yeah, yeah, yeah." But Cam could hear the smile in Reid's tone.

"Plus, you knew I'd jump at the chance once Mom told me that Vi and Adair had discovered an earring from Eleanor's missing dowry."

"One of the sapphires?" Duncan asked. "Wait. Time out. We're talking about one of the sapphire earrings that was probably worn by Mary Stuart on her coronation day?"

"That would be correct," Cam said.

"If I'd known that, I could have gotten away. The local police made an arrest yesterday, and I'm just hanging around to get some fishing in. Remember all the games we played that summer pretending to find those jewels?"

Cam remembered them well, and the discovery of one of them would allow him the perfect cover to visit the castle. There was no need to let his brothers know that the castle might have other problems, not until Daryl had identified Saturday's groom-to-be as Gianni Scalzo.

"When can you get there, Cam?" Reid asked.

Always the organizing big brother, Cam thought. But all he said was, "My ETA will be early morning. I'll check out the security system and find a better place to secure the earring than Angus One's secret cupboard inside the house. That's were they've put it, and I'm betting that most of the population of Glen Loch knows all about that cupboard, including how to pull the lever to get into it. Have a safe flight, Reid. Catch a fish for me, Duncan."

He ended the call and walked toward his car. He had no doubt he could handle providing security for the earring Adair and Vi had found. The real problem he was facing was how he was going to handle Adair.

4

ADAIR'S EYES SNAPPED open. It took a moment for the rest of her mind to register reality. She was in bed and it was still dark. Moonlight poured through the windows. A quick glance at her digital alarm told her that she must have just dozed off. Three-thirty in the morning and something had awakened her.

Not Cam Sutherland. He'd called Vi and said he'd be arriving in the morning. But she could definitely blame him for the hot, sweaty dream that had awakened her shortly after midnight. That was when she'd opened her balcony doors to cool off.

The sound came again and she recognized it immediately. Alba was barking. Adair let out the breath she hadn't realized she'd been holding. Her aunt's room was in the west wing on the other side of the main staircase, and Vi had mentioned the dog was waking up and barking during the night for no apparent reason. So far she'd managed to sleep through Alba's nightly ritual.

Not tonight. That's what very little sleep, a lightning strike and the discovery of a priceless sapphire earring would do for you. But they were going to keep the discovery under wraps. That's what her father had advised when

Aunt Vi had called him. And he'd said he was going to call Reid to let him know so that arrangements could be made to check out the security at the castle. In the meantime, she and Vi had hidden the earring away in a place that was as good as Fort Knox—Angus One's secret cupboard.

Alba continued to bark.

Adair stared up at the ceiling. She'd already lost enough sleep. She didn't need a dog robbing her of the rest of it. She was about to burrow her head beneath the pillow when she heard something else.

Not a bark. More of a…what? A creak?

Jumping out of bed, she padded softly to the door, opened it and listened hard.

Nothing.

Even the dog had gone silent. Aunt Vi had probably quieted her.

She stood there and counted to one hundred while she told herself it was nothing. The castle had never had a break-in. And Vi had assured her the latest updates on the security system had been installed.

But then she recalled how the dog had barked shortly after they'd found the earring. Alba had sensed someone or something in the hills above the stone arch. And she had been holding the earring in her hand. If there'd been someone up there lurking or spying, they'd been in a perfect position to have seen it.

Turning, she paced back into her room and checked the time. Three-forty. Then she strode back to the door and debated going downstairs. To what? To search for an intruder? Barefoot and weaponless?

No way. But there was no way she'd be able to fall back asleep either. She looked around for a weapon. Where was a large brass candlestick when you needed one? Settling on a sizable stoneware pitcher, she grabbed the handle and crept softly into the hallway.

At the top of the stairs she paused, listening again.

Nothing.

There was half a flight of stairs to a landing where tall stained glass windows filtered the moonlight. Once she reached it, she would be visible to anyone below in the foyer. She had to chance it. Taking a deep breath, she moved quickly down the stairs, rounded the curve of the banister, then slipped into the shadows and flattened her back against the wall.

She made herself take slow, silent breaths—in and out—while she counted to one hundred again. And listened. Nothing moved in the large, open foyer below. Nothing made a sound.

As seconds ticked by, she began to question whether or not she'd imagined the noise she'd heard earlier. It was an old house, she reminded herself.

She was ready to go back to her bedroom again when she heard something. A definite creak this time, as if someone had stepped on a board.

Seconds later, she heard it again.

Her heart thudded against her rib cage and she tightened her grip on the handle of the pitcher.

Security system or not, she was not alone in the house. She scanned the foyer again but the shadows didn't budge. Step by step she started down the stairs. Slow and easy, she told herself. At the bottom she paused and listened again. To her right was a door that opened into the dining room, and an archway that led to the west wing that housed the library and the kitchen. To her left was a door that led to the main parlor.

Wood scraped against wood, and this time the creak was loud and familiar. Adrenaline spiked and her heart thudded even harder as she pinpointed the sound. The main parlor. And she knew exactly what was making it.

Someone was breaking into Angus One's secret cupboard where she and Aunt Vi had put the earring. Temper surged through her, pushing fear aside. She was not going to let anyone steal that earring.

She moved quietly toward the door to the parlor and saw that it was ajar. The crack wasn't wide enough to see inside the room. For a couple of seconds she debated what to do. If she called out, asked who it was, she'd alert them.

Not her best move.

The creaking sound came again, then the scrape of wood against wood. Then nothing.

Except for the footsteps. The carpeting muffled them, but they were getting closer. No time to debate her best move. She climbed onto the seat of a chair flanking the door and raised the pitcher over her head.

The opening in the door slowly widened. She stopped breathing. When the figure stepped into the foyer, she brought the pitcher down hard on his head.

He fell like a tree and the pitcher clattered and rolled across the wooden floor until it thudded into a wall.

He wasn't moving a muscle. And he was big. The foyer was a good twelve feet wide and the man's body filled a great deal of it.

Was he dead? Had she killed him? Her knees went so weak she nearly tumbled as she climbed down from the chair.

He moaned.

Relief had her sitting down hard in the chair. Not dead. She drew in a deep breath and the burn in her lungs told her she needed the oxygen.

The figure on the floor moaned again, then his hand snaked out, grabbed her ankle and jerked. She fell hard, the impact singing through her as he rolled on top of her and crushed her beneath him.

He was even bigger than she'd first thought. Still she fought. She went for his face but he blocked the move and pinned her hands over her head. His chest was like a slab of rock. So were his thighs. When she tried to kick he scissored his legs, trapping hers. Finally she screamed, but the only sound she mustered was a squeak.

"Princess?" Releasing her hands he levered himself up, taking some of his weight off her.

Shock was her first response. It was dark in the foyer but she knew that voice. And there was only one person who called her that. "Cam?"

For a moment neither of them moved. Adair felt as if her mind had become a clean slate, and something was happening to her body. All the fight had gone out of it and it was softening, sort of molding itself to his. Flames ignited at every contact point.

His body seemed to be growing even harder. She was intensely aware of every plane and angle, and the thrill of lying there beneath him was so much better than she'd ever imagined in her fantasies. His mouth was close, too. She could feel the warmth of his breath on her lips.

Panic spurted. She had to do something. Push him away. But her muscles seemed paralyzed. And her brain wasn't doing much better.

She was going to have to rely on her mouth. "Get off of me."

When he rolled away and rose to his feet, Adair realized that she'd never said anything more contrary to her desire. She'd wanted him to continue to lie on top of her; she'd wanted his mouth on hers. She'd wanted him to touch her the way he had in the dream she'd had a few hours ago. She'd wanted...

Stop, she said to herself.

Get back down here, she wanted to say to him.

"I'm going to have a hell of a headache in the morning, Princess. Are you all right?"

The easiness of his tone and his use of the nickname he'd given her helped her to gather her thoughts. So did the fact that he'd backed a few steps away and didn't offer her his hand as she stood up. If he had...

Don't go there.

"I'm just fine." That was a total lie. She still couldn't feel her legs, but she managed to fist her hands on her hips. "I'll be a lot better once you answer some questions. First, what are you doing breaking into the castle in the middle of the night *and* into Angus's secret cupboard? Second, how did you even know about that cupboard? It's a MacPherson secret. Last, but not least, where is the earring?"

The barrage of questions made Cam smile. Even in the dimness he could see the flash of fire in her eyes. The heat they'd generated together a few seconds ago threatened to erupt again. He'd been right about the hair-trigger effect she'd have on his senses. It had taken all of his control to get up when she'd told him to. Every cell in his body had been focused on kissing her. And he'd have wanted to do a lot more than that. He still did. He was a man who trusted his impulses, went with them. In two quick strides, he could...

As if she sensed his intentions, she took a quick step back. "Are you going to answer my questions or not?"

She was close to the stairs and if his memory was correct, she was fast. If she ran she might get away. He might be able to let her.

It took a wise man to know when his first impulse wasn't his best one.

"Well?" She tapped her foot.

He held up a hand. "It's taking me a few seconds to process all of the questions. If you ever decide to give up the wedding destination gig, the CIA will hire you. They can always use a good interrogator."

"I could use some answers."

"I'm here because your dad and my mom called Reid. They thought that one of us should check out the earring and the security system. I made much better time than I expected to, and I didn't want to wake you."

"So you broke in?"

"I decided to check out the security system and the earring without bothering you and your aunt Vi. The system is pretty good. It would take a pro or someone with a buddy on the inside to get through it. And since your dad mentioned that you'd put the earring in Angus's secret cupboard, I just wanted to check and see if it was still there. It was."

"How did you know about the secret cupboard?"

"My brother and I convinced your sister Nell to show it to us years ago. And I was a bit worried about how 'secret' it was."

For a moment she said nothing. He felt the pull between them even more strongly than he'd felt it seven years ago, and he knew she felt it, too.

She turned and started up the stairs. "I'll show you to your room."

"Wait." He turned to pick up his duffel, and his hand collided with something else. A stoneware pitcher. It had to have been what she'd clubbed him with. "Way to go, Princess. I've never been taken out by a pitcher before."

"My pleasure," she said as she led the way up the staircase.

"I'll bet." But he didn't say it out loud, nor did he let the chuckle escape as he followed her.

"You're willing to share your recipe for these delicious scones?" Bunny Maitland sprang from her chair, excitement clear in her voice.

"I'll do more than that," Vi said. "I'll demonstrate. Follow me."

Adair watched her Aunt Vi usher Bunny Maitland out of her office right on schedule and willed away the headache that was throbbing at the back of her skull.

Then she shifted her attention to Rexie. The bride-to-be hadn't talked much during their meeting.

There hadn't been much chance for anyone to talk while Bunny was sharing the good news like a weather reporter on a sunny day. The wedding would go on as scheduled. A good night's sleep with all that magic mountain air and quiet—blah, blah, blah—had settled Rexie's nerves.

Adair sorely wished the "magic" air had settled her own. Fat chance of that after her run-in with Cam, which had fueled more fantasies than the ones she'd already written down.

She hadn't been able to catch more than a few winks of sleep. Not with her mind racing at full speed, imagining what might have happened if she hadn't let him up from the foyer floor.

Thank heavens her arms hadn't been working.

Too bad her arms hadn't been working.

Adair pressed a hand to her stomach in an attempt to quell the heat that had centered there, but it was already radiating out to her fingers and toes.

Cam had clearly felt nothing at all. According to Aunt Vi, he'd left her a note that he'd left the castle early to visit the library in Glen Loch. Research on the missing sapphire jewels. He was obviously totally focused on his purpose in coming to the castle.

And she had to focus on hers. Reaching for her mug, she took a long swallow of her cooled coffee and shifted her full attention to Rexie. She wasn't sure how long Vi could distract Bunny, and this might be her only opportunity to discover what was bothering the young girl.

The best description Adair could come up with for the expression on Rexie's face was resignation.

So she asked the question that she might not want the answer to. "Rexie, do you want to marry Lawrence?"

"Of course." The answer came quickly but Rexie didn't meet her eyes.

Not good.

"Why do you want to marry him?"

Rexie's eyes lifted to hers. "Because I want to do something right. I messed up my first marriage because I didn't choose the right person. Lawrence is perfect for me."

The fact that Rexie's answer sounded memorized only increased the intensity of Adair's headache. "How is Lawrence perfect?"

"My father and mother like him—he's been such a good friend to them. And our marriage will help solidify the merger between Maitland Enterprises and Banes Ltd. This is my chance to help with that. My duty. Lawrence has already bought a beautiful estate for us on Long Island. He has memberships in two very prestigious golf and tennis clubs nearby. He's going to hire a pro to help me improve my game. And his estate has a stable. He's going to let me keep a horse. I used to show horses when I was younger."

Adair studied Rexie. As she'd listed all the advantages of marrying Lawrence Banes, it reminded her of all the reasons she'd listed for herself when she'd decided to date

Baxter DuBois exclusively. Of course, he'd pointed them out to her. They'd already teamed up on several projects at the office, and becoming a "team" outside the office would only enhance that. It would put them on the fast track for promotions. And the plan had worked at first. But then Bax's career had begun to advance faster than hers.

She hadn't seen it at first because she'd trusted him. More than that, she'd trusted her own judgment. It wasn't until she'd had that final meeting with her supervisor that she'd learned how wrong she'd been. Bax had been taking all the credit for their success, even for the last client that *she* had brought in. She'd trusted him, and he'd dumped her the same day she'd been fired. He'd explained in his email that it might tarnish his image at the company if he continued to be seen with her. She of all people had to know how important perception was in the cutthroat world of career advancement.

She certainly did now. In Rexie's perception Lawrence Banes was the perfect husband. Was he? "Rexie, are you in love with Lawrence?"

Panic flashed into the young girl's eyes. "If I marry him beneath the stone arch, I will be. And I'll be happy. Won't I?"

Adair heard Bunny's voice, her aunt's laughter. She needed more time with the young bride-to-be, and she needed some help. "Why don't we go down there right now? You didn't have time to check it out yesterday—what with the storm and all. That way you can get a better feeling about it."

"Could we do that?" Rexie smiled for the first time since her arrival at the castle.

"Follow me." Adair rose and quickly led the way through the open French doors. The path to their right led around the front of the house to the gardens. With any luck at all, Vi would distract Bunny long enough that she could get what she needed from Rexie. Perhaps Rexie would get what she needed, too.

The morning was a beautiful one, the sky blue, the breeze cool, and this early in the morning the sun had risen just high enough in the sky to shoot bright lances of light off the surface of the lake. Pansies bordered the path and behind them peonies bloomed in various shades of pink.

Wesley Pinter, Glen Loch's gardener and landscaper, a man who'd been handling the maintenance of the castle's gardens since she was a child, was unloading the last planter from his truck. She noted he'd settled them temporarily on either side of the stone arch. The chairs that they'd set up for the rehearsal the day before were still there and Adair led Rexie to the first row. She gestured her into one and sat beside her.

Then she cut to the chase. "Were you in love with your first husband?"

Rexie tensed. "Mummy says it was infatuation. My therapist says we were just too young. We rushed into it and we weren't right for each other. Coming from the same kind of background helps to ensure compatibility."

A wave of sympathy washed over Adair. Those were Mommy's words or a therapist's, not Rexie's. She laid a hand on the younger girl's arm. "Tell me what happened?"

"Why? It's over. My divorce became final six months ago, and Barry returned his signature on the papers by overnight delivery. I'm no longer Mrs. Barry Carlson. I took my maiden name back as soon as I could." There was a trace of grief in her eyes, a mix of anger and hurt in her voice. Not good.

"Where is Barry now?" Adair asked.

"In Montana. His family owns a horse farm there, and his mother opened a wildlife refuge. We met while he was finishing his degree in veterinary medicine at Cornell. I was a freshman, and I fell in love with him the first time I saw him. I could actually feel my heart take a tumble. He said it was the same for him. We got married as soon as we could. Barry insisted on that. He comes from a religious family and he didn't want me to just move in with him. We didn't have time to do a big wedding thing. We didn't even tell our parents right away. I sometimes wish we'd never had to."

"That's when the trouble started," Adair said.

Rexie sighed. "They were so upset. My father was furious, my mother hurt and disappointed. Barry's family wasn't happy, either. Especially when he told them that he was going to get a job in the East."

"What happened next?" Adair prompted.

"We started trying to make everyone happy again. My father got Barry a job in a very upscale, very busy veterinary practice on Long Island, and my mother threw a huge wedding reception for us at her country club. But I could see that Barry wasn't happy. Neither was I. I barely saw him, and when I did we always argued. And when his grandfather died he went back to Montana."

"You didn't go with him?"

Rexie's eyes grew shiny with yet-to-be-shed tears. "He didn't ask me to. He promised he'd come back. But each time he called he made excuses. An ailing horse, then sick animals at the refuge forced him to extend his stay. Then he sent me a letter saying that we'd made a mistake and he wanted me to handle the divorce on this end."

A Dear Jane letter, Adair thought. Why was it that men were so lacking in class?

"After that he wouldn't even take my calls. I'd leave a message but he'd never call back." She blinked back the tears and her voice became very firm. "I made a huge mistake marrying Barry. This time I want a guarantee. Can you give me that?"

"I can promise you that getting married here will give you your best shot at it."

"Rexie?" Bunny's voice was accompanied by the sound of Alba's bell.

Adair turned to see Aunt Vi bringing up the rear of the small parade. Bunny was a bit breathless when she reached them. "We have to leave for the city now if we're going to make the final fitting on your dress. Then we have to get ready for your bachelorette party tonight."

"Our gardener just unloaded the planters," Adair said. "Can't you stay long enough to give them your final approval?"

Bunny waved a hand in the direction of the flowers. "I'm sure they'll be lovely. But we need to make this fitting. The dress has to be perfect. It's a copy of the one I wore on my wedding day. She's going to wear my veil, also."

Bunny gave Rexie a little push toward the car, then spoke in a very low voice to Adair. "My plan is to keep her busy and focused on the wedding. Your job is to make sure that there are no more glitches on this end. She and Lawrence chose this place against my wishes. They've refused to change venues at this late date, and I've agreed because I want my daughter to be happy."

Bunny's smile didn't quite reach her eyes as she continued. "I'm sure you want her to be happy, too. That way I'll have only good things to say about Castle MacPherson."

With that, Bunny hurried to catch up with her daughter. Seconds later the flashy red convertible sped out of the driveway.

"Well, well. There's a core of steel beneath that sweet magnolia exterior," Vi murmured as she stepped to Adair's side. "And none of the 'glitches' yesterday were your fault. You certainly can't be blamed for the storm, nor for the fact that the groom-to-be was late and distracted."

"Well, Bunny can't very well get angry with Mr. Banes. Not when she's so desperate to make sure this wedding takes place."

"What did you learn from Rexie?"

"Her upcoming marriage will be a marriage of convenience."

"Whose convenience?" Vi asked.

"Exactly. There's money involved. And I think Rexie's still in love with her first husband." She glanced through the stone arch. "I've always believed there's a lot of power here. I suppose we should just leave it to the legend. But I'd like to know more about what's going on with the Maitlands and Banes that makes this wedding so important."

"You're still afraid we might have a runaway bride on our hands."

"Or lightning may strike again." She was beginning to think that the stone arch might have more power than she'd ever realized.

5

THE CAR CAME out of nowhere, flying over the crest of the hill and then smacking down to barrel toward him. Cam's reflexes, honed by his training as well as the experience of battling two brothers as he grew up, kicked in immediately. The narrow dirt road in front of him led to only one place. The castle. And it was going to be very tricky to negotiate past the red convertible shooting toward him at race car speed.

Tall pines with trunks as thick as a giant's thighs pressed close on either side. Thanks to that summer he'd spent playing on the castle grounds, he had some knowledge of the road.

The blonde driving the convertible didn't. Or she wouldn't be speeding. She was risking her own life as well as her passenger's. Keeping his hands steady on the wheel, he set his foot gently against the brake.

Tires squealing, the convertible ahead skidded, swerving wildly from one side of the road to the other. Dust spewed and he prayed for it to settle. He couldn't edge over yet. He was going to need a wide angle when he made his turn. And he prayed it was coming up soon.

With a bare twenty feet to spare, Cam spotted the slight

break in the trees he was looking for and pulled his steering wheel hard to the right. His car fishtailed, bringing it parallel to the trees before it straightened and shot forward. Narrowing his eyes, he pressed his foot gently on the brake, aiming the front of the car right between the two giant pines. He thought of the biblical image of trying to squeeze a camel through the eye of a needle. Impossible. But the car whispered through and bumped its way into a shallow gully. He was grinning as he managed to stop just short of the next tree.

Jumping out of his car, he ran back to the road to check on the convertible just in time to see it disappear around a curve. Son of a...

But it hadn't been a son of a bitch driving that car, he reminded himself. It had been a woman and she'd been in as much of a hurry as the Disney villain Cruella de Vil when she'd been hunting down those hundred and one Dalmatians. Turning, he glanced up the hill where dust still hung in the air. There was only one place she could have come from, since the road dead-ended at the castle.

Then he glanced back down at his car. He'd managed to avoid crashing it, but he was going to need a tow out of that gully. The castle was still a couple of miles off. A nice hike if you weren't in a hurry. There was a part of him that was anxious to get back there. But there was still a part of him that was practicing avoidance where Adair was concerned—something that he'd been doing for the past seven years.

Old habits died hard. He'd left a note for Vi near the coffeemaker in the kitchen that he was going into Glen Loch to let the sheriff know about the earring. He'd also wanted to stop by the library to refresh his memory about Eleanor's missing dowry.

Both were perfectly valid excuses—but not the only

ones he'd had for wanting some time before he came into contact with Adair again.

Cam moved quickly down the incline and grabbed the bag the librarian had given him to carry the books and copies he'd made at the library. His mother had used the Glen Loch library when she'd researched the missing sapphires for her book. It was always best to look at the primary data. Partly that was his CIA training talking and partly it was the curiosity he'd always had about those missing jewels. When he and his brothers had played with the MacPherson girls during that long-ago summer, his favorite game had been "pirates." And the treasure they'd always sought had been the sapphires.

His mother's research had never turned up even a hint of what had happened to them. But the proof of their existence had always been right there in the main parlor of the castle in Eleanor Campbell MacPherson's portrait. When his mother had been researching, she'd picked up on the story that the sapphires had once been worn by Mary Stuart and that they'd been Eleanor's dowry. But exactly when or how they'd disappeared was still a mystery. And no one knew exactly how the sapphires had come into her family's possession. The mystery had always drawn him. And it was one of the reasons his mother was in Scotland right now researching the Campbells and MacPhersons on that end.

And mysteries surrounding the sapphires had drawn someone else to the Glen Loch library that morning. The librarian, a tall, spider-thin woman with sharp eyes, had greeted Cam warmly as soon as he'd identified himself, telling him that she remembered when his mother had brought him and his brothers to the library that summer when they'd first visited the castle. And she'd been very willing to tell him about the stranger who'd come in the moment she'd unlocked the doors. He'd asked for help in locating anything on the missing MacPherson sapphires. She couldn't give Cam a name, but she'd described the stranger as a man with brown hair, a receding hairline, mid-forties, with a portly build. He'd been wearing khaki slacks, a baseball cap and glasses. And he'd printed copies of some of the materials he'd accessed on their new computers.

There were two things that bothered Cam about the guy. His timing and the fact that he was a stranger. His own reason for visiting the library, besides avoidance, was the fact that he knew one of Eleanor's earrings had surfaced. Was it just a coincidence that a stranger had dropped by the library the same morning to gather information on the missing sapphires?

Cam had never put much faith in coincidence. He wasn't even willing to bet that it was some kind of coincidence that had pulled him back to the castle right now.

Shouldering the bag, he started up the hill. Adair was different for him. He'd sensed it on a bone-deep level seven years ago when she'd stood beneath the stone arch with him while their parents exchanged vows. He trusted his gut instinct, something that had always served him well at his job. And working for the CIA had also honed his skills at analyzing data. What he'd learned from his encounter with her on the floor of the foyer last night was that avoiding her hadn't changed a thing. She was still different for him. And he still wanted her.

This time he couldn't just leave the way he'd done when he was twenty-two. He was stuck here until he'd done what their father had requested and thoroughly checked out the security. For now, he'd made sure that the earring was safe. But there was someone else who was suddenly interested in the sapphires. And there was still the job that Daryl had asked him to do. His boss hadn't contacted him yet, which meant he still hadn't been able to definitely identify Saturday's groom as his longtime nemesis. But Adair or Vi might know something about Lawrence Banes that would help him out.

So avoidance time was over.

He hadn't even kissed her yet. But in spite of the fact that he had a lot on his plate, he wasn't sure that he could resist the urge to taste her for very long. And they weren't twenty and twenty-two anymore.

Last night he'd lain awake in the guest room reliving what it had felt like to have every soft curve and angle of her body pressed against his, and the devouring heat, the churning in his gut, that the contact had triggered. The sensory memories had kept him from sleeping for hours.

Cam reached the top of the hill the red convertible had shot over and caught his favorite view of the lake, the sturdy castle with its terraces and balconies nestled in the tall pines, the lush gardens and the blue lake glimmering like a sapphire below it. From this spot, he could even see part of the stone arch. He knew how to do his job. What he still had to figure out was what he was going to do about Adair. And as he started down the hill to the castle, he wondered if he had a choice.

ADAIR DRAGGED THE last potted plant into position, then stepped back to survey what she'd been able to accomplish since the departure of the Maitlands. Her aunt had returned to the kitchen to work on the groom's cake. The mix of lavender hyacinths and purple irises offered a stark contrast to the gray stones, and the colors would pick up the tones in the maid of honor's and flower girl's dresses.

The physical exertion of moving the pots into place had helped her get a clearer perspective on Rexie's wedding.

Focusing on a task and finding a solution had always been one of her strengths. But that skill hadn't worked for her in Chicago. In hindsight, she could see that she'd been so focused on the projects she'd been doing with Bax that she hadn't picked up on the fact that he was taking all the credit for them.

Maybe she just didn't have good judgment when it came to men. Which made it very good that her attraction for Cam Sutherland was one-sided. And he'd no doubt be leaving today. How long could it take to check out their security and reassure her father?

Pushing the thought out of her mind, she backed up to the first row of chairs and sank down. She had a wedding to pull off and she was going to do her best to ensure it went forward. Everyone wanted it to, including the bride.

In her mind, she pictured the bridal couple standing beneath the arch and imagined what she hadn't seen yesterday. The minister saying, "You may now kiss the bride." Rexie wrapping her arms around Lawrence and kissing him.

Visualizing your goal was essential to achieving it, just as important as writing it down. That was business school 101. It had been hammered home in every self-help book she'd read, every entrepreneurship course she'd taken. Even her ex-boyfriend, Bax, had talked about it. He probably believed that she'd been axed and he hadn't because of his superior visualization skills.

Or had the problem been that she hadn't been able to "see" what he'd been doing? Maybe she hadn't wanted to see reality. Instead she'd wanted to believe in the fantasy she'd created in her mind of their perfect partnership.

Focus. Bax was history, and Cam soon would be. What she needed to concentrate on right now was the upcoming wedding. The fate of her new business plan depended on its success.

Closing her eyes, she summoned the image to her mind. *Rexie kissing Lawrence. Rexie kissing Lawrence.* Digging into Rexie's first marriage to Barry was not her problem. Pulling off the second one to Lawrence was. Slowly her imagination delivered. Pretty Rexie, her blond curls all pulled up with pearls threaded through them. And the groom, holding her close.

Keep your focus. Wait for it.

The image grew clearer and closer. A tall man with lean, chiseled features and sandy-colored hair finally lowered his mouth to Rexie's.

But he definitely didn't look anything like Lawrence Banes.

Cut. Stop action.

Adair snapped her eyes open, but the stranger's mouth had been brushing Rexie's before she'd pushed the image out of her mind.

She pressed her hands to her temples. *Think of something else.* A quick glance at her watch told her that she still had forty-five minutes until her next appointment. A prospective client who'd called first thing that morning. Nathan MacDonald. He'd been driving through the mountains and stopped at the diner in Glen Loch, and the patrons had been talking about the upcoming wedding. He and his fiancée were looking for the ideal place to schedule their own wedding. Adair had set him up for a brief tour.

She dragged one of the chairs out of its straight line and propped her feet on it. Leaning back, she closed her eyes and just for a minute, she made her mind go blank. She concentrated on the sensation of the warm sun on her face, smelled the scent of fresh mulch, pine and flowers.

In the distance she heard the rumble of the lawn mower and much closer the chattering of birds, the hum of bees.

As she let herself drift, another image filled her mind. It was blurry at first, but as it slowly came into focus she saw that *she* was standing beneath the arch, not Rexie. And the man holding her? Hard to see in the shadows cast by the stones. But she grew steadily warmer as the features slowly sharpened in her mind—the dark unruly hair, the lean face with its slash of cheekbones. Familiar.

The hands were not so familiar, but as they gripped her waist and pulled her closer, pleasure rippled along her nerve endings. She tipped her head up as he lowered his. He was close now. In another second, his mouth would... With a sigh, she let herself sink into the kiss.

THE INSTANT THE driveway curved past the stone arch, Cam spotted Adair. He'd taken three steps toward her before he realized he was moving. She had her feet propped up on one chair, her eyes closed, and her head resting on the back of another. A wiser tactic might have been to turn around and continue on to the castle. He wanted to ask Vi to give him her take on the bridegroom in the upcoming wedding.

But a good agent took advantage of every opportunity to gather all kinds of data. It had been too dark in the foyer last night to get a good look at Adair. This was his chance to study her. If he could pinpoint just what it was that drew him, he might be able to figure out a solution.

While he crossed to her he had time to refresh his memory of that neat, trim little body. She was wearing shorts, and he noted that the legs were longer than one might expect in someone of her slight stature. She was still slender, but the hint of curves she'd had at twenty-one had fully matured.

As he drew closer it was her face that drew his gaze and stopped him in his tracks. Maybe it was because he'd never seen her asleep before that he hadn't noticed how fragile she looked or how really delicate her features were. He'd nicknamed her "Princess" to annoy her, but he'd never thought of her as one. Princesses needed white knights to rescue them and fight their battles. When he was ten he'd never thought of her that way. If he'd had to play with a girl, he'd figured she was okay. She could handle herself.

But right now, nestled on that chair with a curl tumbled across her cheek, she looked vulnerable, someone a white knight would want to protect and cherish. And it wasn't a fire he felt spreading through his blood; it was something much warmer. He found it nearly as intriguing as heat. And probably more dangerous.

Still, he ignored the impulse to walk away and said, "You've got to stop slaving away like this."

The voice had her eyes snapping open but her mind still clung to her dream. In it, Cam's mouth had been on hers. Now reality registered slowly. Blearily, she made out long legs clad in worn denim. She shifted her gaze upward, taking in the narrow waist. The chambray shirt was rolled up revealing muscled forearms. A big man, she thought, broad shouldered. One hand gripped the handles of a canvas bag; the other was long fingered and resting on narrow hips.

But even when she managed to raise her eyes all the way to his face, it took a second for her mind to fully focus. Her heart had already begun to race, her body to weaken before recognition slammed into her.

"Cam?" She blinked again, trying to gather her thoughts.

"Forgotten about me already, Princess?"

"Adair," she corrected automatically. Some of her

strength returned. "I must have fallen asleep." And he'd sneaked into her dream just as he'd sneaked up on her when she was asleep.

Asleep?

She shot a panicked look at her watch, then let out the breath she'd been holding. If she'd drifted off, it hadn't been for long. But her brain still seemed to be operating on a three- or four-second delay. She got to her feet and found herself craning her neck to meet Cam's eyes. She hadn't had to do that in the foyer last night. Not when she'd been face-to-face with him on the floor.

The Sutherlands were all tall, but she could have sworn that Cam had grown even taller since she'd seen him last. And he'd changed. At her father's wedding he'd still been partly a boy. Now she was facing a man, and as she looked into those blue eyes her throat went dry and something was happening to her knees.

No one had ever affected her this way. She had to get a handle on it. She couldn't afford to let some man befuddle her brain again. Pushing past the dryness in her throat, she said, "What are you doing here?" Brilliant. "I didn't hear your car."

"Some bat out of hell ran me off the road."

Her eyes widened. "When?"

"Half an hour or so ago. Red convertible. She looks like Marilyn Monroe and drives like she's in the Indy 500?"

Adair nearly smiled. "That was Bunny Maitland, the MOB, otherwise known as the Mother of the Bride." She ran her eyes over Cam again, stifling the urge to linger. "You look fine. How's your car?"

"Needs a tow." He set down the canvas bag. "But I enjoyed the walk. Is Blondie the MOB in this Saturday's wedding?"

She narrowed her eyes. "How do you know about the wedding?"

"Sheriff Skinner mentioned it when I dropped in to tell him that you and Vi had discovered one of Eleanor's earrings. According to him, the whole village is talking about the rich couple from Long Island who are getting married here. They're hoping they'll spread the news about what a lovely spot you have here and increase the tourist trade."

"That's the plan," she said. "What's yours? Has our security system passed muster?"

"Not yet." Cam had to bite back a smile. This was the Adair he remembered, just a little on the pushy side. "Can you show me where you and Vi found the earring?"

"Over here." When she started to tug on one of the heavy pots overflowing with blooms Cam grabbed the other side to help her shift it.

Pointing to the rocks and stones that still lay strewn at the base of the arch, she said, "This is where we assume Alba found the earring. We heard her digging around on this side, but we didn't actually see where she found the leather pouch. Aunt Vi and I searched through these stones to see if we could find the rest of Eleanor's dowry, but they're essentially where we found them."

Cam swept his gaze over the side of the stone arch. It was about ten feet long and the height stretched to about ten feet. The rocks varied in size and offered enough small ledges and handholds that he and his brothers had scaled the thing countless times. In fact they'd even had team relay races with the girls. He'd always chosen Adair because she hadn't been afraid.

Angus One was supposed to have built it himself but Cam figured he'd had some help lifting the bigger slabs, and he must have possessed a natural talent for engineering. The thing had stood there for over two hundred years.

"Did it take a direct hit from the lightning?" he asked.

"If not, it had to be close. We were in the middle of the wedding rehearsal, and when the storm thundered in, the closest place to take shelter was here. Most of the wedding party was already beneath it. When the lightning struck, the impact was enough to tear the bride out of the groom's arms and into the minister's."

Cam pictured the scene in his mind. "If I were the groom I might take it as a warning and back out."

"He's not the problem," Adair said.

Cam studied her. "He's not?"

She shook her head. "The wedding will solidify some business arrangement that he has with the bride's family. So her parents are on board, too. And the bride is depending on the legend to provide her happy-ever-after. It's all good."

Her words were saying one thing, her eyes another. Adair's eyes had always been so easy to read, and she was worried. She might have more to worry about than she knew. The business merger side of the wedding fit in perfectly with Gianni Scalzo's M.O., and that argued Daryl's instinct might be right.

He shifted his gaze to the stones and spotted a small crevice where the rocks and smaller stones might have fallen out. Dropping to his knees, he slipped his hand inside.

"There's nothing there," Adair said. "I told you Vi and I already checked to see if there was another pouch."

"There are more loose stones." He pulled one out, half the size of his palm, and poked his hand in again. He pulled out an even-larger one.

Adair dropped to her knees and tried to get a look around his shoulder.

"I can't quite finesse this next rock, but I can feel space behind it." He grunted, then said, "Yeah, I think we've got something here."

6

"WHAT? Another pouch?" Adair asked.

"Can't tell. First I need to get past this stubborn rock. If I could just get a good grip..."

"Let me." Moving on her knees, she wiggled closer until she was practically plastered to his side. "My hand's smaller."

She slid it into the opening. When his rough palm slid over her skin, heat streaked to her toes. "Get your hand out, so I can try—"

He turned his head and suddenly they were face-to-face. All she saw were his eyes. They were so dark, the color of the sky near twilight.

"Try what?"

The words had her dropping her gaze to his mouth. That was exactly what she wanted to try. The taste she'd sampled in her dream hadn't been enough. When his hand wrapped around hers, she felt the heat sear through her right down to her toes. His lips were close, only an inch away. All she had to do was eliminate that small distance and all her dreams and fantasies would become real. She would finally feel the pressure of his lips; she could finally taste him. Lord, she could smell him. Soap and water and something that was different. Male. Just breathing in had the intense and achy need inside of her sharpening. And it wasn't going to go away. Unless—

"We should—" she began.

"Yeah."

Later, Cam wasn't sure who moved first. All that mattered was that their lips brushed, met. And clung. Heat exploded at the contact and spread like electricity along a hot wire. Then, each scrape of teeth, each tangle of tongues upped the wattage.

He streaked his free hand up her side and around to cover her breast. Then he pulled his other one out of the crevice so that he could hold her fully against him.

Blood roared in his ears. Desire hammered at him with a sharpness he'd never felt before. He wanted her, wanted to peel those clothes away and explore every curve and angle. He wanted to feel her skin grow hot and moist beneath his hands. He wanted her beneath him again. No woman had ever taken him this far with only a kiss. In another moment...

Cam had no idea what finally gave him the strength to pull back. They were both panting. Nothing else marred the silence other than the distant hum of a hedge trimmer, a soft breeze at the tops of the pines.

"That was..." She broke off as if at a loss for words.

"Yeah." That was the single one he could latch onto.

"Crazy."

"Insane," he agreed. And Lord help him, if he could just kiss her again, he'd take the straitjacket.

"You and me. It would be a mistake."

"Probably." He moved his hand to the back of her neck and fastened his mouth on her throat. Her scent was stronger here—fresh flowers and sunshine. He found it incredibly erotic.

"We can't... We have to... Stop."

That one word had him struggling to latch onto a thin thread of control. He raised his head, but he couldn't take his eyes off hers. And he saw himself completely enclosed in the misty green.

"Just one more taste." She fisted a hand in his hair and drew his mouth back to hers. Heaven, she thought. And hell. His mouth was so skilled and much more potent than she'd ever imagined. With his teeth and tongue he nibbled, then devoured, seduced and then possessed.

Oh, she'd expected the heat, welcomed it as it flooded through her again. But the intensity of it—the way it sizzled and burned, singeing, then melting everything in its path. That was so new. So amazing. She wanted more. She wanted to crawl right into him until she dissolved and the terrible need inside her eased.

When he ran his hands down her sides, she felt his touch in every part of her body. Her breasts ached, her thighs trembled. When he drew back she wanted to cry out from the loss.

"Adair, we have to finish this inside."

"Inside?" The word floated into her consciousness through a thick fog. "Finish this?" Finally, his meaning penetrated. Shock tore through her when her first reaction was to say yes. Still, it took all her focus to say, "No."

He dropped his hands and sat back down on his heels. She had to brace herself against the stone arch or slide bonelessly to the ground.

What had she been thinking?

The answer to that was pretty simple. She hadn't been thinking at all. Except about what it might be like to kiss Cam. And now that she knew...

"We have to think about something else." Fast, Adair

thought. "We were searching for the rest of Eleanor's jewels."

"Right." It shocked Cam that the jewels had slipped entirely from his mind. There'd been no room for anything but Adair. Before this, desire had always been enjoyable, simple. It had never slashed through him until the wanting had been…everything.

Think about something else.

Edging farther back, he dragged his gaze away from her and glanced at the crevice.

"You think the rest of the jewels might be in there somewhere, don't you?" she asked.

"I think it's odd that you only found one earring."

"Okay. So we need to check it out. But this time we take turns. I'll go first and try to loosen the stone you were working on. Once I have it out, you can work on the next one."

Cam had to smile as he edged even farther away and gestured her toward the small hole. "This is only a temporary solution to our problem."

She shot him a look over her shoulder. "I know. But I need to think about it."

"Go ahead." He knew the value of analyzing data. He just wasn't sure how much time either of them had for that.

Adair reached in and slid her fingers around the edge of the rock. Then she began to wiggle it back and forth. "It's coming. Slowly." She had to use both hands to pull it through the opening. Then she moved carefully out of his way. "Your turn."

The instant Cam reached in, his fingers brushed against something with more defined edges than a rock. Dipping one of his shoulders, he leaned closer to the opening so that he could get a better grip. Carefully, he slipped his fingers over the top and finessed his thumb beneath it. Then he tugged.

"You've got something," Adair said.

"A box, I think. But it's snugged in pretty tight." His fingers slid off, but not before he felt it give a little. He tried again, and this time it moved a couple of inches.

"It's coming." The next sixty seconds seemed to go by in slow motion, but inch by inch he tugged and pulled the box closer and closer until he could get a good enough grip to drag it all the way out.

Once he set it on the ground between his knees and hers, Adair could do nothing but gape at it. She was looking at the box she and her sisters had buried seven years ago.

Cam fingered the tiny padlock. "Shall I do the honors?"

"No." Snatching it up, she clutched it to her chest, out of harm's way.

"That lock is pretty flimsy, but if you'd rather, I have a set of lock picks in my room."

"No. You can't open it. Eleanor's jewels aren't in here."

Cam studied her for a moment. "And you know this because?"

Her cheeks burned with embarrassment. "Because my sisters and I buried this box on the night our parents were married. What's in here is very private."

"Really?" Cam looked at the metal box.

Adair frowned at the intrigued look on his face.

"How in the world did you get it in there without coming across the pouch with the earring?" he asked.

"We didn't bury it on this side. We loosened some stones on the inside of the arch."

"And you're not going to let me see what's inside?"

Adair narrowed her eyes. "What don't you understand about the word *private?*"

Cam held his hands up, palms outward. Adair was about to say more when they heard a car on the graveled drive.

Adair shot to her feet. "That's my one o'clock appointment." She looked down at her dirty knees and scowled. She didn't even want to think about what her hair might look like. No time for a shower. But she could at least tidy up.

Amused, Cam watched her bolt into the garden and race for the back door of the castle with a death grip on the mysterious metal box. Not that it was any of his business.

But secrets had always intrigued him.

Whatever they were, they'd caused a very pretty blush to spread up her neck and across her face as she'd warned him off. Discovering people's secrets was one thing he was very good at, and working in the CIA had honed that particular skill. One way or another, he was going to find out what was in that box.

But there was other business he needed to take care of. Taking out his cell, he punched a number he always kept on speed dial.

Daryl's voice mail picked up. That meant that he must be totally engrossed in his investigation. Cam passed on what Adair had told him about the Banes/Maitland wedding being connected to come kind of business merger. And he wished he didn't have a gut-deep feeling that the bride might not be getting her happy-ever-after on Saturday.

TEN MINUTES LATER, Cam found Viola MacPherson exactly where he'd expected to find her—in the kitchen. And she was frosting a delicious looking cake. For a moment as he stood in the doorway, he was transported back in time to his tenth summer. Except for her gray hair, Viola looked the same.

The dog was new. The medium-sized mixed breed was out for the count in a rectangle of sunshine not far from Vi's feet. The security system they had was pretty good, and he trusted that Vi and Adair were religious about securing the castle at night. And the dog provided added protection. But like most people, when they were home during the day they left doors such as the one he currently stood in open.

"I don't suppose I could talk you out of a piece of that cake," he said.

She whirled, set down her knife and beamed a smile at him. "Cam."

The dog raised its head, jingling the bell around its neck, and rose to its feet. Vi signaled the dog to sit as she moved to wrap her arms around Cam. The gesture tightened something around his heart.

"You seem taller since the wedding," she said as she stepped back.

"You're not." He glanced over her head at the cake.

"Don't even think about it. That's the groom's cake for the wedding on Saturday. The whole affair is dicey enough without the cake disappearing. Sit. I'll pour you some iced tea, and I have fresh scones."

Grinning at Vi, he sank into the chair she'd pointed at. "The MOB ran me off the road just before I got to the twin pines."

Vi ran a quick look over him. "You look okay. The car?"

"Not a scratch. I talked to your gardener, and he said he'd tow it out and have the young guy working for him drive it up here."

"Wes is a good man." She poured two glasses of iced

tea, piled scones on a plate, then carried everything to the table and sat down.

"When I spoke with Sheriff Skinner, he suggested I tell your gardener about the discovery of the earring. The news is bound to leak out—it may have already." He told Vi about the stranger who'd visited the library. "On the days he's up here working, Wes can be on the lookout for trespassers."

Vi nodded. "Are you expecting trouble?"

"After two hundred years, part of Eleanor's dowry has shown up. A lot of people are going to assume that the rest of it is around somewhere. I told A.D. and my mom I'd make sure you and Adair would be safe here." Cam took a sip of the tea and reached for a scone. When the dog moved to his side and plopped her head on his knees, Cam broke off a piece and passed it on.

"I can put her out on her leash," Vi said.

"She's fine," Cam said. "How long have you had her?"

"Six months. I went to the animal shelter to find a good watchdog, and the moment I saw Alba I had to bring her home. She's deaf. But even though she may not hear in the same way you and I do, she senses things."

"What made you want a watchdog?" Cam asked.

"A feeling more than anything. I started waking up in the middle of the night. I never really heard anything, but now Alba wakes me up with her barking. I still never hear anything else—even after I settle her down. But I feel safer."

"What about Adair? Has she ever heard anything?"

"No."

"No signs of intruders or a break-in?" Cam asked.

"No. And I've looked. Nothing is missing." Vi tapped the side of her head. "You're going to tell me it's all up here."

"Not at all." He also didn't intend to tell her how easy it might be for a professional to get past their security system. But usually a break-in was a onetime thing. This had been going on for some six months—long before the earring had been discovered.

Cam slipped another bite of scone to the dog and turned to his original purpose for seeking out Vi. "Adair's worried about this wedding on Saturday, and you said earlier it was dicey enough."

By the time he was biting into his third scone, not counting the one he'd shared with Alba, he had Vi's version of the story. "So in a nutshell, what you've got is a bride who wants a guarantee for a happy-ever-after because she didn't get that the first time around. You've got an MOB pressuring you and Adair to make sure everything runs smoothly on Saturday. A business deal hangs in the balance, and the bride-to-be might be still in love with her first husband."

Vi nodded.

"How does Adair feel about all of this?" Cam asked.

Vi sighed. "She's torn. She wants our wedding business to succeed more than anything since that horrible fiasco in Chicago."

Cam frowned. "What fiasco?"

"She was working with a young man who charmed her into believing that the two of them could make an unbeatable team both inside and outside of the office." Vi used her fingers to put "unbeatable team" in quotes. "Then he passed her projects on to upper management as his own. Long story short, he's still working there and she isn't. And he dumped her on the day she got her pink slip."

"Bastard." The anger Cam felt didn't surprise him. What did was the bitter coppery taste in his mouth. Jealousy?

"Adair has always succeeded at everything she's set her

mind to. She believes that if she pulls this wedding off on Saturday, the future of Castle MacPherson as a wedding destination spot will be assured. If not…"

It was Cam's turn to frown. "If not, she'll find another way to accomplish her goal."

Vi smiled at him. "Of course she will. You know that and I know that. But she has to rediscover that about herself."

Cam didn't like the fact that he might play a role in ruining the wedding. If Banes turned out to be Scalzo… For now he decided to put it out of his mind and pursue another question that was lingering there. "Adair was showing me where Alba discovered the earring, and we came across a metal box with a little padlock. She wouldn't let me see the contents."

Vi laughed. "Of course she wouldn't. She and her sisters used to write down their secret dreams and aspirations and put them in that box from the time they were little kids. When they were teens they came up with the idea of burying it behind some loose stones in the arch as a way to make them all come true."

Interesting, Cam thought. But it wasn't a childhood dream that had made Adair blush and become so territorial about the box.

And solving the mystery of what was inside the metal box was not why he was here at the castle either. "Do me a favor, Vi?"

"I have no idea what's in that box."

He smiled. "I want to know where your bedroom is with regard to the rest of the house."

At the question in her eyes, he continued, "I'm wondering if there might be a reason why you and Alba are having your sleep disturbed and Adair isn't."

"I'll do better than tell you," Vi said. "Let me show you."

7

"THANK YOU SO much. My fiancée will have to approve, of course, but I'm enchanted with this place."

Smiling, Adair shook the hand Nathan offered. She liked him. He wasn't a handsome man, but he had intelligent eyes and a blustery, enthusiastic energy that she found engaging. She guessed he was in his mid-forties. His waistline had begun to spread a bit and gray had begun to dull both his mustache and beard as well as his nearly shoulder-length red hair. This was his first marriage and he wanted to do it up right.

"I'll look forward to hearing from you," she said.

He patted the professional-looking camera that hung at his side. "You will. These pictures are going to sell the place to my sweetheart."

Adair certainly hoped so. The man had taken enough of them. She watched him walk to his car, and when he reached it and turned back to her she gave him a final wave.

She'd shown him the gardens, the ballroom, and at his request she'd even taken him into the parlor to view Eleanor Campbell MacPherson's portrait. Nathan had mentioned he remembered reading about Eleanor's missing jewels in the *Times* a while back.

Even though they were not offering the use of the main parlor in any of the wedding packages, Adair supposed she might as well put it on the regular tour from now on. If the word got out that one of Eleanor's earrings had shown up, she figured more than one potential client was going to ask to see the portrait.

She thought the appointment had gone well, considering that more than once she'd felt her mind wandering. Back to that metal box and the fantasies she and her sisters had buried in it all those years ago.

And back to Cam Sutherland and that kiss they'd exchanged.

As the last little whirlwind of dust settled from Nathan MacDonald's parting car, Adair turned and walked back to her office. She was going to have to figure out what to do about Cam. And herself.

Closing the door behind her, she strode to her desk, sank into her chair and stared at the small metal box. She was responsible for this. It had been her idea to write out the fantasies and bury them in the stones. And she wasn't going to blame the champagne. Earlier that day when she'd met Cam's eyes beneath the stone arch, her heart had raced, her breath had stopped and her whole world had tilted.

So for the first time in her life, she'd done something rash. And now it was coming back to haunt her.

Big time.

She could be the poster girl for the "Be careful what you wish for" warning. What was worse is that she wanted that wish to come true.

She pressed her fingers against her lips and found them warm. Now that she'd seen him again, lain beneath him and kissed him until her brains had practically leaked out of her ears, she didn't want the fantasy anymore. She wanted the reality.

The problem was she did not have time to indulge in the reality of having an erotic adventure with Cam Sutherland right now. There were so many things she had to check on to ensure the success of Rexie Maitland's wedding. Pulling a pad of paper closer, she began to jot down notes. Aunt Vi was handling the cakes and overseeing the catering service. The firm she'd hired would arrive early Saturday morning to set up the tables in the ballroom. Cocktails and champagne would be served on the terrace overlooking the lake.

When Adair realized that her eyes had shifted to the box, she focused on her list again and wrote at the top: (1) Check in with the florist. (2) Call Rexie.

Tonight maybe. She'd sleep better if she knew that the young bride-to-be's nerves had definitely settled.

(3) Call first husband Dr. Barry Carlson.

Adair dropped her pen and stared at what she'd written. Call Barry Carlson? Why was she even thinking of doing that? Hadn't she decided Rexie's first marriage wasn't any of her business? Then she thought of her conversation with Rexie that morning and the look in the young woman's eyes when she'd said, "He refused to talk to me." Hurt that Rexie hadn't recovered from yet.

Dammit. She fisted her hands on her desk. It wouldn't hurt to look up the phone number. Rexie had mentioned that Barry's parents had horses. Lifting her notebook computer out of the top drawer, she booted it up and searched for the Carlson Horse Ranch in Montana. A few clicks got her to the web page.

And there he was—Dr. Barry Carlson. To her surprise, he looked vaguely familiar. She thought of those moments where she'd been sitting in front of the arch, using her visualization technique to picture Rexie kissing Lawrence Banes. But the man her imagination had summoned up had looked a lot more like Barry than Banes.

No, that couldn't be. She'd never met Barry Carlson. Her mind was just playing tricks on her. When she caught herself jotting down the phone number of the horse farm, she dropped the pencil and stared at her hands. They were playing tricks on her, too.

And it was all because she was trying so hard not to think of that box and Cam Sutherland. So much for avoidance.

Thoroughly annoyed, she pulled it toward her. Cam had been right about the lock not providing a challenge. Over the years the flimsy thing had rusted enough that she was able to pull it away with one jerk.

Taking a deep breath, she opened the lid. And there they were—the three compartments with folded sheets of different-colored paper in each one. It had been Nell's idea that they use different-colored paper for privacy. She'd chosen yellow. That night she'd written on a legal pad and the sheets lay there right on the top of her section.

Unable to resist, she took her fantasy out and shoved aside her day planner and To Do list. Then she unfolded the pages and spread them over the surface of her desk. There was always the chance that she'd find her adolescent fantasy amusing or even laughable. Perhaps just reading it would put it in perspective and she could get her focus back.

But her lips didn't so much as curve as she read the words she'd written so long ago. She barely recognized her own handwriting. She'd written at such a rate of speed, wanting to keep up with the images that had flooded her mind. They were as compelling now as they'd been seven years ago. And they were even more erotic.

Being swept away by a stranger had been a fantasy of women for years. And she'd learned in a female studies class she'd taken freshman year that the fantasy was grounded in what had been the reality of many women's lives for thousands of years.

But the fact that it had been *her* fantasy that long-ago night—the fact that it was that particular fantasy that had gripped her imagination and flowed out of her pen had shocked her then.

It shocked her right now.

The pages she'd written that night were all about being transported by a man and by the danger of the adventure. As she skimmed the words, she could see that she'd incorporated elements of *Romancing the Stone* and *Indiana Jones,* and even the first Jason Bourne movie.

The most exciting thing she could think of that night was being swept up in a life-threatening adventure with a man. The sex had to be hotter when it was layered with fear and the adrenaline of the chase. It had always seemed to be that way in the movies.

And it wasn't just the lure of danger and excitement that had captured her imagination, it had been the man she'd imagined doing everything with her.

Cam Sutherland.

He was the man she'd imagined lying beneath. He was the man who'd kissed her, touched her and thrust into her.

And now that she wasn't operating on imagination, now that she'd had a taste of reality and experienced the promise of what might lie beyond the kisses they'd exchanged...

Her blood heated, raced, and something deep inside of her tightened.

She pressed a hand against her heart to keep it from

pounding right out of her chest. How could she possibly reconcile her response to him with the woman she was and had always told herself she wanted to be?

Women who ran off with sexy strangers, chased bad guys in cars, dodged bullets and plunged into mountain streams were...just...not her.

She was organized, goal oriented. She made lists and liked to follow them. She made five-year plans for heaven's sake. So what if her first one had crashed and burned? That only meant she had to concentrate fully on the next one. There was zero room in her life for unplanned and unwanted adventures. Lightning strikes and missing jewels were not on her agenda. And neither was hot-as-you-can-imagine sex with Cam Sutherland.

And if all that were true, why was she losing her mind every time he touched her?

She dropped her head in her hands. Before she did something really stupid, she had to think about this. She had to get some kind of a handle on it and come up with a plan.

Gathering the papers on the desk, she put them back into her compartment and closed the lid. She had to think this through, and her favorite thinking place had always been at Tinker's Falls. After replacing the lock, she tucked the box into her bottom drawer. Then she hurried out through the French doors and headed into the woods.

CAM SLIPPED TO the side of the French doors just as he saw Adair start toward them. When he'd arrived on the terrace she'd had her head dropped in her hands. The posture was so unlike her that he'd stopped short to study her. Once again her vulnerability tugged at him. Had her meeting not gone well? He'd glanced around the room, then arrowed back to the flimsily locked metal box. Was that what was upsetting her?

For a moment all he'd wanted was to go to her, to draw her to her feet and just hold her. But before he could give in to the impulse she lifted her head and gathered up the papers on her desk, put them back in the box and tucked everything away in a drawer.

When she had risen from the desk he'd stepped to the side of the open doors, and now he watched her cross the terrace and head to the path that led to the woods. The energy in her movement, the intent way she'd left the office, reminded him more of the Adair he thought he knew than the woman he'd glimpsed with her head in her hands.

He waited only until she disappeared before he stepped into her office. The space was roomy and might have once served as a second parlor. There were bookcases flanking a stone fireplace, double doors on another wall that opened into the entrance foyer, and to the left, French doors that led into the main parlor.

He had a theory now about why Vi and Alba were having their sleep disturbed and Adair wasn't, and it also might explain why neither of the women had noticed anything missing from the castle. Vi's room was situated over the castle's library, a two-floored room that hadn't been used in years. It still housed a dust-covered but extensive collection, some of it dating back to Angus One. According to Vi, the last person who'd used it for any length of time was his mother. That room was where she'd spent most of that summer when he and his brothers were ten.

If the castle did have an intruder and he or she had confined themselves to the library, that might explain why Adair's sleep had never been disturbed. But that theory opened up a lot of questions. Such as, why would someone want secret access to the library? Why not do what his mother had done and simply ask permission?

Or maybe he was totally off the track. But he'd wanted to talk to Adair about it. More, he'd wanted simply to see her. For a moment he found himself torn. There was a part of him that wanted to follow her and another part that was curious about the contents of the mysterious box.

And he might not get another opportunity like this one. Glancing over his shoulder, he checked to make sure that she was out of sight. Then he crossed to her desk. It was typical Adair, with its day planner and To Do list. He skimmed the first two items, then studied the third. *Call first husband—Dr. Barry Carlson.*

So she really was torn about the wedding. Perhaps her gut instinct was giving her a message similar to Daryl's. Something wasn't right about Lawrence Banes.

He opened the bottom drawer and lifted out the box. She hadn't bothered to latch the tiny lock, so he removed it and opened the lid.

It was divided into three compartments. One was stuffed with folded pieces of colored paper: the one on the left with yellow, the center one with blue and the final one with pink. Organized. He recalled what Vi had said about the three girls writing down their hopes, their goals and their dreams on colored papers and burying them in the stones.

That scenario didn't fully explain the acuteness of Adair's embarrassment. Cam removed the folded colored papers on the top of each section and spread them out on the desk. The date in the top right-hand corner told him that each had been written on the night that his mother had married A. D. MacPherson seven years ago. Each was a different length, each was in a different handwriting, but they had one thing in common. The title at the beginning of each one read: "My Fling With My Fantasy Man."

Totally captivated, Cam sat down in the chair and picked up the first one.

Half an hour later his view of the MacPherson girls had undergone a transformation. They might have been young when they'd penned the fantasies, but they'd had active and inventive imaginations. Though they'd definitely been written from a woman's viewpoint, he'd been caught up in each of the fantasies. Enough that he could use a cold shower.

He'd immediately recognized Adair's as the first one he'd read. It had been on yellow paper. Not that he hadn't confirmed his judgment by checking the handwriting against her To Do list. That neat block lettering was a dead giveaway. And of course he'd had to read the other two. A good agent had to be thorough and look at all the data.

They'd each been incredibly arousing. Sex on demand, any time you want it, any way you want it, no strings, no holds barred. He could relate to that fantasy, all right. And the other one was interesting, too—a string of scenarios in which the woman was the seductress and always the initiator. Every man's secret dream.

They just weren't Adair's. Hers was the longest and it was all about erotic sex on the run with that added spice of adventure and that hit of adrenaline. Even when they were kids she'd had that desire for adventure. It was why he'd been drawn to her and why he'd wanted to partner with her instead of her sisters. Because she could take a dare and she could issue one.

He glanced down at the block letters on the yellow pages. She'd certainly issued one now. He wanted to make the fantasy real for her, for them both. They were adults now—why not enjoy the fantasy and each other before they had to go their separate ways?

Right. Rising, he paced to the French doors, then walked back to the desk. You didn't work six years for the CIA and not learn that things were seldom that simple.

He glared at the box. Curiosity was a very dangerous thing. It had killed the cat and it had caused Pandora to inflict chaos on the world. Now he had a feeling that it was going to play havoc with the life he'd built for himself. One that he'd been totally satisfied with until he'd seen Adair again.

He folded the papers, put them back in the proper compartments and replaced the box in the drawer. Then he strode out of the office, across the terrace, and followed the path Adair had taken into the woods.

8

ADAIR STRIPPED OUT of her T-shirt, then slipped her sandals off and wiggled out of her shorts. Beneath, she wore a white string bikini that she'd put on that morning just in case she had a chance to get a swim in before lunch. Then she folded her clothes and placed them on a flat rock at the edge of the water. The pond that lay at the base of Tinker's Falls was one of her favorite places on the castle property. The falls themselves were part of a stream that wound its way down the mountain. Twenty-five feet above, the water narrowed, then dropped in a clear curtain to the pond below. Behind the curtain there was a secret cave.

For as long as she could remember she and her sisters had used the place as their own private swimming pool. Flat ledges of rock flanked the top of the falls on either side and made perfect spots for sunbathing. Or diving. She walked to the edge of the pond.

It was about thirty feet long and twenty-five wide. And it wasn't really a pond. In sixth grade science she'd learned that it was a deep plunge pool left behind when the glaciers had melted. There was plenty of room for the lap swimming she'd done at college.

Anticipating the shock, she dived into the water, then

surfaced with a thrilling shiver and set out for the other end. A vigorous workout usually helped her think clearly, and Lord knew she could use a little clarity.

What in the world was she going to do about Cam Sutherland? Reaching the other end of the pond, she tucked, curled and then pushed off with her feet. So much was riding on establishing the reputation of Castle MacPherson this summer. She might have come up with the business plan on the fly, so to speak. In fact, she might never have thought of the potential business opportunity at the castle if she hadn't been fired. But lightning strikes and possible runaway brides aside, she was beginning to enjoy the wedding business. It was exciting and satisfying to help young couples plan the most important day of their lives. She even liked the constant challenges. Not that she wanted any more lightning strikes.

She just didn't have time for a complication like Cam. She surely didn't have time for some adolescent action/ adventure fantasy. Did she?

She let the question hang there for three more laps before she ruthlessly shifted her attention to another equally pressing problem. Barry Carlson, Rexie's first husband. There was a good chance that Rexie was still in love with him. Was Barry still in love with her? She let herself consider that for five more laps. Calling Montana to find out what Barry's feelings were was about as smart as kicking a hornet's nest.

And just about as risky as thinking seriously about giving in to her attraction for Cam Sutherland. How in the world had she become a woman who was so attracted to living on the edge?

But wasn't that one of the reasons she was so drawn to Cam? He was dangerous for her in a way that Baxter DuBois had never been. Bax had represented what she'd convinced herself she wanted in a man. Someone who had the same goals and wanted the same lifestyle. She'd felt comfortable with him. Maybe that's why she'd let him talk her into the team partnership idea. And look how well that had turned out.

She'd never felt comfortable with Cam. He'd always stirred her, aroused her, challenged her. And those feelings had grown even more potent over time. What else could he make her feel? She wanted to know how much more there was.

This time when she tucked, curled and turned, she struck out for the left side of the falls where she'd left her clothes. Reaching it, she pulled herself out of the water and climbed up to the ledge of rock that bordered one side of the falls.

The sun was hot overhead, the wide, flat rock warm beneath her feet. Inviting. A quick glance at her watch told her that she could afford to stay long enough to dry her swimsuit. That would be practical.

And it struck her suddenly that there had to be a practical way to solve the situation with Cam. They both wanted the same thing. A fling. Why couldn't she just look at it like a wedding plan, a short-term event that fulfilled both party's dreams? And then life would go on.

As she stretched out on her back, using one arm to shield her eyes, she started working out the approach she would take with Cam. But it was kicking hornets' nests that she was thinking of when she fell asleep.

CAM STOPPED AT the edge of the trees to watch her climb out of the pond. She looked like some kind of nymph with her hair slicked back, the water sliding off of her body. She wore nothing except two scraps of white that had his mouth going dry as dust. And her legs—he'd gotten some hint of them before, but with nothing marring their length they were making him sweat.

She was strong, he noted as he watched her climb to the top of the ledge. When she rose to her feet and stretched her arms upward, it wasn't a nymph he thought of—but a goddess. Her guts he'd never doubted. But the fearlessness he saw now and the vulnerability he'd glimpsed earlier were new. And they fascinated him.

He'd done his best to avoid thinking about her for years. Now he couldn't stop. And he wanted to know more. Still he didn't move toward her.

Everything should be simple. She wanted him and he wanted her. More than that, he was beginning to learn the way her mind worked. He thought he knew the approach to take. A practical one.

So why wasn't he moving? No woman had ever made him hesitate before.

Dammit. He strode forward into the clearing and circled the pond, approaching the ledge from the back side. When he made it to the top he stopped again, surprised to see that she appeared to be sleeping and hadn't heard his approach.

He glanced around. There was no one upstream. The trees pressed in on all sides of the falls, offering at least the illusion of privacy. His approach as well as any noise he'd made climbing up the rocks had been totally masked by the crash of the falls below.

He shifted his gaze back to Adair and stopped thinking of anyone or anything else. It had only been a matter of a few hours since he'd kissed her. The desire to do so again had only grown as he'd imagined her in each of the girlish fantasies he'd read. That was a hell of a lot of foreplay for a man.

And what she was wearing—or more specifically, not

wearing—nearly had his tongue hanging out. Her skin was the almost-translucent color of fine porcelain and nearly all of it was showing.

He dropped to his knees, not fully recognizing that's what he'd done. Then he simply couldn't stop himself from touching her. Reaching out, he traced one finger over her cheek, then down her neck, and he felt the shock of the contact shoot through him with the intensity of a flame. All thought of his simple straightforward strategy slipped from his mind as he continued to run his hand lightly over her skin.

ADAIR DREAMED SHE was floating in a bubble of warm, sleepy pleasure. Something, the sun perhaps, was caressing her skin, stroking gently over her cheek and down her throat to trace a delicate path along the curve of her breast. She sighed even as she shifted, arching slightly into the caress. She could picture the languid fingers of sunlight stroking over her, arousing and seducing so delicately as they moved, as soft as an artist's brush, over her rib cage to her waist and then down her thighs and back up. Slowly, achingly, the pleasure built layer upon layer upon layer as the pattern was repeated.

Warmth gradually edged into heat—little flicks of fire that raced outward along her nerve endings and seeped deeper and deeper into her center. She was melting now, and she wanted to. It was no longer the sun she imagined stroking her but a lover's hands.

And the caresses were growing more demanding. When the fingers brushed again along the curve of her breasts they seared her skin. Her heart raced and she commanded her eyes to open. Blinded by sunlight, she couldn't bring anything completely into focus. But as she reached to ease the burning sensation, her hand collided with, then gripped, a solid masculine one.

Reacting purely on instinct, she sat straight up; fisted her other hand and aimed an uppercut to his chin. The figure grunted, then landed on his behind just as she recognized her opponent. "Cam?"

"Hey!" He rubbed his jaw with one hand and extended the other, palm outward, to forestall another blow. "You seem to be determined to hurt me. First a stone pitcher and now an uppercut."

"Sorry." Maybe it was the mix of shock and admiration on his face or his rueful tone, but she had to struggle to turn a laugh into a hiccup. "Really, I'm sorry." She covered her mouth with both hands as the laugh broke free. "So sorry."

"I'm glad I'm such a source of amusement."

The dry tone had her stifling another giggle. "You might stop sneaking around."

"Where's the fun in that?" But he smiled.

Then after a beat of silence, he said, "I'd apologize for touching you while you were asleep, but it would be a lie."

The words made her vividly recall exactly what he'd been doing before she'd decked him, and she remembered what she'd decided before she'd drifted off. Straightening her shoulders, she clasped her hands together in her lap. "I don't want an apology. I've been thinking, and I believe I have a solution for what's going on between us."

"I'm all ears." He had a solution, too, and he'd been about to demonstrate it just before she'd decked him. "But make it fast. I can't guarantee how long I can keep my hands off of you."

"It's simple really," she said, her voice a little breathless. "We're both very busy right now. What we need is a plan."

"A plan?"

"Yes. When couples come to the castle to plan their weddings, the first thing we do is sketch out the parameters before we negotiate the details. But in our case I think we both want the same thing—a short-term, mutually satisfying physical relationship with no strings and no complications. After all, in a few days you'll be going back to Washington and I'll be working on the next wedding here at the castle. So while we have this time together I'm suggesting we have what my friends in Chicago always called 'buddy sex.' "

"Buddy sex?" All Cam could do was stare at her. She might just as well have punched him again. What she was suggesting didn't fit with her fantasy at all. Was it the arrangement she'd had with the boyfriend back in Chicago? The thought made him furious and brought that coppery taste back to his mouth.

"Surely you've heard of it." Her tone was pleasant, earnest. "No expectations. No worries about tomorrow. Just hot and very satisfying, on-demand sex between two people who want each other but don't have time for all the problems of a relationship. It's perfect for us."

For the first time he noted that her hands were clasped tight, her knuckles white. Nerves.

The fact that she was feeling them was enough to ease his temper as he met her eyes again. "You've had some experience with buddy sex, I take it?"

She lifted her chin. "And you haven't?"

"You're right. I have." He'd not only had those kinds of relationships in the past. He'd made them his specialty. But buddy sex hadn't been the fantasy she'd written on those yellow pages seven years ago. He was more certain of that than ever. Reaching out, he covered her clasped hands with his. "Tell me what you really want, Adair."

"I want to get everything straight going in so that nei-ther of us has unrealistic expectations. No hurt feelings. Do we have a deal?"

The bastard in Chicago had hurt her. That meant she deserved an honest answer. "The problem is there are no guarantees. Certainly not in my line of work. And I'd bet that in spite of the fact that you like to cross all your t's and dot your i's, weddings are pretty unpredictable, too."

"Yes, but surely we can—"

"Try." He smiled as he pulled her to her feet. "Let's try this." He gripped her hips, lifted her, then strode to the edge of the ledge and jumped.

They hit the water. The cold hard shock of it, the thrill of it, sang through her system as they plunged deep and then deeper. She had no choice but to hold fast and go along for the ride. She didn't want any other choice. By the time their momentum slowed and they kicked upward, her heart was racing, her lungs burning.

When they broke through the surface of the pond they were eye-to-eye. His were so dark and glittered so fiercely that choice was snatched away again. All she could do was sink into them just as she had into the water.

"Breathe," he said. But he barely gave her time before his mouth crushed hers and they went under again.

With one arm, he kept her pressed against him and with the other he touched her—sliding his hand from the nape of her neck down her back to her hip. But his touch was no longer gentle the way it had been when she'd been half dreaming. It was hard and possessive—the way she'd always fantasized it would be. In spite of the icy water surrounding them, heat coursed through her system. She wanted nothing more than to melt into him. Nothing.

They were going to drown. The thought flickered like a guttering candle in some part of his brain, but Cam-couldn't find the strength to heed the warning. The completeness of her surrender had him falling hard and fast into a world where there was nothing but the two of them and this terrible need she'd triggered in him.

His foot hit the bottom before he got enough of a grip on reality to kick them both back to the surface. This time when they broke the water, they were gasping and coughing. Latching onto a glimmer of sanity, he kicked to the side of the pond and pinned her against the rocks.

"Look at me," he said.

When she did, he skimmed a hand possessively over her hip and slid two fingers into her. He watched those misty green eyes darken and glaze as she embraced him and gasped his name.

"I've imagined doing this to you," he murmured as he began to move his fingers, coaxing her into a rhythm. "There's more I've imagined." So much more. He was going to show her.

She was moving faster now. He knew he could take her right here against the side of the pond. Fast and hard. The speed might ease some of the terrible pressure building inside of him. But there was so much more he wanted to give her. More he wanted to take.

Then her mouth nibbled at his neck, her teeth scraping his skin in fast, greedy bites, and he felt his control start to slip. He wanted everything. The hitch of her breath, that husky, hungry sound she made each time he stroked his fingers in and then out, in and then out. And the heat—her body seemed to be on fire, and he wanted nothing more than to be consumed by the flames. Then she clenched his fingers, her hungry mouth fastened on his, and they slipped beneath the water again.

The climax streaked into her, blasting a path from where his fingers pressed through every pore in her body.

Reeling from it, she kept her mouth fused to his and demanded more. He gave her more and more as they sank into a dark primitive world and unspeakable pleasure peaked again.

"Breathe," Cam ordered when they reached the surface.

Her lungs burned when she did.

"Got to get you out of here."

Water was streaming down her face, but he filled her vision, the dark hair slicked to his head, the fierce eyes.

"More," she said.

He groaned and shifted his face away when she tried to capture his mouth. "We could die."

"The...cave," she managed between nips at his bottom lip. "Behind...falls."

Cam remembered then. He should have before. And thank God she had. But getting there was going to be a challenge. Holding her close, he struck out for it, using his feet to propel them toward the waterfall. But those long, silky limbs were tangled around him, trapping him. Her mouth was so close, the waterfall so far.

Talk, he told himself. And then he thought of her fantasy and whispered in her ear. "I'm a pirate. For weeks, I've watched you from my ship. Every day you come down to the rocks to bathe and then rest in the sun. I've watched you, fantasized about you, wanted you."

"Yes," she breathed in his ear.

"You've felt my eyes on you."

"Yes." She nipped his earlobe, and Cam nearly lost his focus again. "I've wanted you for so long. Kiss me again."

Not yet. He didn't dare. Carefully, he negotiated the waterfall and they reached the shallower water that bordered the cave. "Today I couldn't resist you any longer, so I swam ashore to make love to you. To make you mine."

Finally, his foot hit a rock ledge and he found enough

balance to shift both of them onto the floor of the cave. She lay beneath him now just as she had in the foyer the night before. He could see her eyes, the dark gleam of them and nothing else as he lowered his mouth to hers.

Now he could explore all those flavors that he'd only sampled before. But as he tasted her, as the flavors poured into him, he felt as if he were drowning again.

And he couldn't seem to get enough. Each time he changed the angle of the kiss, he discovered something new. Beneath the incredible layers of sweetness, there was the darker flavor of desperation. The richness of her tastes, the depth of them, ignited a fire in his blood that started in his gut and radiated to the tips of his fingers. Fingers that trembled as they drew away the wet material that still clung to her breasts.

Her body arched up, offering more, and he had no choice but to take. He told himself to go slowly, to savor when what he craved was to devour and possess. Her skin was slick and so hot that it burned his lips as he moved them down the slim column of her throat. Using teeth and tongue, he lingered at her breasts, teasing, torment-ing, taking. He felt her heart beat against his lips and his own nearly stopped.

Each time she shuddered, each time her nails dug into his shoulders, a fresh thrill threatened to shatter his sys-tem. Wherever he touched or tasted, her response was so generous, so beyond his experience, he could never have imagined it. Ever.

"Cam."

He could barely hear his name above the rush of the waterfall and the pounding of his blood, but he knew she thought only of him. The power of that nearly pushed him beyond reason. But each time he thought he had to end it, he found more to tantalize him. Lured by the slim line of her torso, entranced by the dip at her stomach, he journeyed lower.

When he found himself blocked by the strings of her bikini, he ripped it away.

"Cam."

Adair had no idea whether she said the word aloud or whether she'd only managed to shout it in her mind again and again. It echoed through her, streaming through her veins, filling her. The story of the pirate and of the woman who'd waited replayed in her mind. Their longings, their needs, couldn't possibly be as great as hers. She'd waited so long for Cam. For this.

Too long.

No one had ever made her feel this way. The need he'd triggered was primal and raw. It terrified her. Electrified her. And just when she thought he couldn't possibly take her further, he did. Each press of his fingers, each scrape of his teeth showed her how much more there was. And when he used them on the skin of her inner thigh, she cried his name again and arched her hips upward. And he pressed his mouth to her core.

The orgasm tore through her, erupting again and again in aftershocks that only left her craving more. There was only Cam, the taste, the smell, the sight of him. When he rose above her again, she fisted her hands in his wet shirt and ripped it apart. Buttons flew.

"Again," she demanded. Then, as desperate as he to taste, to touch, to devour, she rolled with him across the floor of the cave. Legs and arms tangling, they struggled to pull down his wet jeans and strip off his shirt.

"Hurry," she demanded.

"Trying to."

But when she would have dragged him back on top of her, he sat back on his knees and shifted her so that she was straddling them. Then he dug his fingers into her hips to hold them still. They were eye-to-eye, nearly mouth-to-mouth. "Protection," he managed to say.

He dug his fingers into the pocket of his jeans and they fumbled with the condom together.

"Hurry," she said again.

He watched her eyes and nothing else as he lifted her hips and plunged inside of her. She was all he knew, all he wanted. And in that moment, she was everything. They moved together then. And when she climaxed, clamping those long legs around him and crying out his name, power and triumph, heady and sweet, streaked to his core.

Then he built the pleasure again, for both of them. Her nails raked his back as he fought against the mists that threatened to blur his vision. He wanted to see her. Had to see her as they both rode a new and towering wave of sensations. Her face beaded with water, her eyes, witch-green, were fastened on his. They trapped him as surely as the lust. He felt something inside of him that wanted to break out, something strong. He tried to hold it back but her name broke free from his lips as he took her with him over the edge.

9

AFTERWARD THEY CLUNG like wet rag dolls against the wall of the cave. They didn't speak. Adair wondered if her vocal cords might have been cauterized by the heat they'd created. She'd known that Cam would be different for her, but nothing in her experience, nothing in her imagination had come close. No one had ever done the things he'd done to her. And she'd never even dreamed of the things she'd done to him. They'd gone so far beyond her fantasies.

And they were real. She'd never felt like this, so weak, so feminine. So totally satisfied.

She sat snuggled on his lap, her arms and legs wrapped around him, her cheek pressed cozily against his. She would have been content to stay just as they were for a very long time.

But that would be dangerous. She'd outlined their relationship quite clearly, and he'd been ready enough to agree there were no guarantees. The important thing would be to stick to the plan she'd outlined and enjoy what they could have together as long as it lasted.

When Cam turned his head and met her eyes, something fluttered right under her heart.

"You know, I have to be honest with you," he said. "I don't think we did that right."

She stared at him. "We didn't?"

"You said you wanted buddy sex—convenient, no harm, no foul. And you nearly killed me."

The mocking note of accusation in his voice caused a laugh to bubble up and break free. "It was your idea to jump off the ledge. You're the one who nearly killed us both."

"Well, maybe we just need more practice. I'm sure we'll get better at it." He was about to prove his point by actions when he heard his cell phone beep. He managed to keep hold of her as he finessed it out of his jeans.

"How did your cell phone survive?" Adair asked.

"Special CIA issue. Waterproof," he said as he glanced at the text Daryl had sent.

Fingerprints of the man who ran a Scalzo-like scam in Oregan match Lawrence Banes's. I'll be joining you soon.

"Important?" Adair asked.

"A friend of mine is close to tracking down an old enemy." What was good news for Daryl was definitely going to be bad news for Adair's wedding on Saturday. But he couldn't even warn her until Daryl was sure. That worry faded from his mind when he glanced up and noticed movement on the other side of the falling water. Lowering his head, he spoke close to her ear. "Don't move. We may have company."

Easing Adair onto a ledge of rock, he pulled up his jeans and found his shirt. Someone standing on the shore of the pond couldn't see into the cave because of the thick fall of water and the darkness. But he and Adair could get at least a blurred image of anyone who came into the clearing.

Two people had. Cam crawled to the far side of the falls where there was a narrow gap between the crashing water and the side of the cave. Pressing his face against the rock, he peered out.

Because of the spray he still couldn't get a clear image. Two men stood at the far end of the pond. One had his back to the falls and stood with one foot propped on a rock, his forearm resting on his thigh. He wore slacks and a white shirt, and he was tall and broad-shouldered enough to partially block the other man's face. That one held a camera with a telephoto lens. He, too, wore city clothes—slacks and a golf shirt. He was shorter and on the chunky side, with longer hair and a mustache and beard.

And they were not happy.

Though it was impossible to overhear their conversation, they were clearly arguing. The man with the camera used his hands in staccato gestures. The other one shook his head vehemently.

"Let me see." Adair pitched her voice low as she wiggled in front of him.

He eased back so that she could try to see through the narrow gap between water and rock. "Recognize either one of them?"

"Maybe," she murmured. "The mist blurs everything, but the man I had an appointment with just before I came out here, Nathan MacDonald—he had a camera. The hair and the build are right. I gave him a tour. He was particularly interested in Eleanor's portrait. He'd said that he'd seen the photo in the *Times* article and he'd love to see the real thing."

"You showed it to him," Cam said.

"Sure. It's not in the regular tour I give, but many people ask to see it."

"How about the other man?"

Even as Cam asked the question, the two men started up the path into the woods. For as long as she could she studied the back of the taller one who brought up the rear. Something seemed familiar, but she couldn't place it.

"No. I don't know."

Cam turned her around so that they were kneeling on the floor of the cave facing each other. "This Nathan Mac-Donald could have decided to come back and take his own private tour of the rest of the estate. But that doesn't explain the other man."

"He mentioned bringing his fiancée back. But I didn't get the idea it would be today. And he didn't mention that his fiancé was a man."

"But their visit could still be legit. He might want to get the fiancé's reaction before filling you in on all the details."

"Yes. And what we saw was just a little lovers' spat?"

"Maybe." The presence of the two men could be perfectly legitimate. But he had the same feeling he'd had earlier when he'd been driving back from Glen Loch, that sense that he should get back to the castle.

"Okay," Adair said, "we've established a semiplausible reason for Nathan MacDonald and his companion to be here with a camera and being a little secretive about checking out the estate. But you're still worried."

"Because we can't be sure how many people know about the earring yet. Vi mentioned to your dad that Alba barked at someone or something in the hills behind the stone arch right after you and she opened the leather pouch."

He filled her in on the stranger at the library who'd been

so interested in Eleanor's missing dowry. "And I think that
someone may have been breaking into the castle at night
for the past six months or so—ever since your Aunt Vi
started waking up in the middle of the night."

Adair frowned at him. "But how? We activate the security system every night. And nothing is missing. We
would have noticed."

"I've been thinking about that. There are times during the day when you deactivate it because you and Vi
are home. You're seeing clients. She's in the kitchen and
wants to enjoy the breeze from the lake. Depending on
their motivation someone could sneak in late in the day.
Or if they have the skill they could bypass the system just
as I did. And maybe whoever it is just needs access to the
castle for a specific reason. Your aunt's rooms are over the
library. She and the dog are waking up and you're not."

"You think someone's looking for something in the
library?"

"My mom spent a whole summer there doing research.
And the *Times* article renewed interest in Eleanor's sapphires. I went to the library in Glen Loch first thing this
morning to look them up and to check out what's available to the public. If I were looking for some jewels that
could be traced back to Mary Stuart, I'd gather data. And
the castle's private library would be at the top of my list
to find more. But I'm just theorizing, posing possible ex-
planations."

Like the one he'd just posed for the two arguing men,
which seemed less and less plausible by the minute. "At
any rate, I'd like you and your aunt Vi to look at the library. Let me know what you see. Let's get dressed."

"Easy for you to say," she muttered. "My clothes are
out there where I dropped them, and you destroyed my

bikini. Not that I didn't enjoy that part. But there's always a price to pay."

"I could promise to make it up to you later."

She grinned at him. "I'll hold you to that."

Vi WAS WAITING for them in Adair's office when they got back. Alba lay at her feet. "Someone broke in here while you were out," she said.

Cam mentally cursed himself as he glanced around the room. He'd noticed the obvious flaws in the security and hadn't acted quickly enough to prevent this. And he'd been so focused on going after Adair that he couldn't recall whether or not he'd even closed the terrace doors.

Adair crossed to her aunt. "Are you all right?"

"I'm fine." She glanced at the two of them. "What happened to the two of you?"

"We took an unexpected tumble into the pond," Cam said. "Did you see who broke in?"

Vi shook her head. "I was putting the last touches on the groom's cake when Alba started to bark and then she ran out of the kitchen. By the time I caught up with her she was scratching on the door to Adair's office. The doors to the terrace were open, and the second I let her in she bolted out through them and just barked for a while. I heard a car start up, but even the dust had settled by the time I circled around to the front."

The driveway had been empty when they'd stepped out of the woods. There'd been no sign of Nathan MacDonald or the man he'd been arguing with.

Vi gestured to the patch of sunlight Alba had stretched out in. "Now I can't get her to leave this room."

"Take a look around, Adair," Cam said as he secured the terrace doors. He'd already taken a quick scan of the room. The metal box was now on her desk and the contents had been overturned. Colored papers littered the floor. As she crossed to her desk, he said, "Is anything else out of place that you can see?"

She turned then and looked around the room, the first time quickly and the second time more slowly. He did the same but he didn't notice anything else that looked disturbed.

"Everything looks fine." Adair gathered up the papers that were scattered across her desk and on the floor and put them into one of the drawers. It didn't look as if any of them had been unfolded. Then, because her knees felt weak, she sank into the chair behind her desk.

"Someone was in here," she said. "And it's not too big a leap to think they were looking for that earring."

She shifted her gaze to Cam. "Someone could have seen you and me this morning when I pulled out the box. I put on quite a show, clutching it and running into the castle with it when my appointment showed up. Nathan MacDonald could have seen me dash for the house with it, and it was right here on my desk the whole time I talked to him. Even if he didn't know about the earring Alba dug up, he might have been curious about the box. That could be the reason he came back."

"Who's MacDonald?" Vi asked.

Adair filled her in on the man's earlier appointment and about the two men they'd seen arguing at the falls.

"If they were the two who did this, it was a crime of opportunity and not very well planned," Cam said. "Let's see if they searched anywhere else." He led the way through the French doors into the main parlor. The portrait of Eleanor Campbell MacPherson hung in place, but the door to the secret cupboard beneath it stood wide open. "Looks like they did."

"The earring—" Adair couldn't finish the thought.

Cam put a hand on her arm. "Sorry. I forgot to tell you earlier. I took it out of there last night as soon as I got here. Angus's hidey-hole was mentioned in the *Times* article, and with the way that news and rumors can be counted on to go viral in this community I didn't want to take the chance of leaving it there."

Adair whirled on him, not sure whether to hug him or hit him. She compromised by shaking off his hand. "You lied last night."

"I told you the earring was safe." He lifted his pant leg and Adair saw the slight bulge beneath the flesh-colored tape he'd wrapped around his ankle. Tapping his fingers against it, he said, "Special waterproof CIA issue tape. Until we get the security updated around here and lay down some ground rules, the sapphire earring's bonded to me. I promise you I'll keep it safe."

In her imagination Adair pictured armed guards at the wedding. "What exactly do you have in mind?"

"What I'm suggesting for now is that we all be more careful about shutting and locking the outside doors to the terraces during the day, and that we activate the security system whenever someone is alone here, like Vi was earlier. I'll call Sheriff Skinner in Glen Loch and let him know what's happened." Cam punched a number into his cell.

Adair began to pace back and forth in front of the portrait. As he relayed the information to the sheriff, Cam watched her. Whatever blow she'd taken when she'd seen her metal box upended or when she'd initially thought the earring might have been stolen, she'd bounced back and now she was totally focused on the problem at hand.

She had a quick mind. It hadn't taken her long to figure that MacDonald might have had a reason to ransack her office. And when they'd been in the pond and his brain cells had completely shut down, she was the one who'd remembered the cave.

"Sutherland, you still there?" Skinner asked.

"Yes." She was distracting him. Taking his mind off business. He couldn't recall a woman who'd ever had that kind of power over him.

"I can spare a man to come out there for the wedding tomorrow—unless you think you need someone tonight."

"Morning will be fine," Cam said. "Thanks."

Then he turned his attention back to Adair. One of the reasons she could distract him was because there were so many layers to her. And each one was so intriguing. There was the woman who'd had the courage to come downstairs last night and hit him on the head with a pitcher. Then there was the woman who'd punched him on that ledge. And the generous and passionate woman who'd met his every demand in the cave. And she'd done more than that. She'd made her own demands, and if she had more he wanted to meet them. There was more to learn about her. More he intended to discover.

"Something doesn't quite make sense here," Adair said. "I can understand that Nathan MacDonald could have just been in the right places at the right times and decided to take advantage. But his knowing about the secret cupboard argues that he has invested a little more time in his research."

Turning to Cam, she waved a hand around the room. "And how does all of this relate to your theory about a person who's been breaking into the castle for about six months?"

"What theory?" Vi asked.

Cam filled her in on his idea that someone might have been making nocturnal visits regularly to use the library. "After you showed me the room this morning I took a quick walk-through, but the two of you have been here for years. I'd like you to take me on a little tour and tell me what you see."

Cam led the way down the hall and ushered the two women into the long, narrow room. A spiral staircase offered access to the balconies that rimmed the second floor. On three walls, bookshelves stretched from floor to ceiling except for the space taken up by a fireplace. The fourth wall was filled with tall windows and sliding glass doors on both levels, and dust motes danced in the afternoon sunlight. Books were everywhere—stuffing the shelves and spilling into piles on tables, chairs and even the floor. Their scent filled the air.

"We haven't used this room in years," Adair said as she walked down the center.

"A.D. locked it up after the girls' mother died," Vi said. "It was Marianne's favorite place. The last time anyone spent any time here was when Beth did her research."

When she reached the terrace doors, Adair turned back to face him. "What are we supposed to be looking for?"

"Evidence that someone has been in here. If I believed Eleanor's jewels existed and I had the time to devote, this would be a good place to start my treasure hunt. I went to the library in town first thing this morning to see what they had, which was easy, as public libraries have a catalog. Everything is arranged in order. That's not true here. It's one of the reasons Mom had to spend so much time here that summer."

The two women went about their task methodically. Adair checked the doors first and found them locked just as he had. "How did this person get in?" she asked.

"There are ways around alarm systems," Cam said.

Adair and Vi split up to start checking the shelves. By

the time Adair got to the end of the room where they'd entered she had noticed exactly what he had.

"There are different levels of dust on the shelves. The farther I go, the less I find—as if he's working his way down the room book by book. Is that what you think this person has done?"

Good eye, he thought.

"Now that you mention it," Vi said, "I can see the same pattern on the shelves over here. And I think I can see where he sits to do his reading."

Cam and Adair joined her in front of the fireplace where a stack of dustless books sat in a pile next to a leather chair.

"So someone has been just coming in here to go through this library book by book to find Eleanor's dowry? Who in the world has that kind of patience?" Vi asked.

"A true treasure hunter—someone who believes that Eleanor's necklace and earrings are somewhere in the castle or on the estate. Maybe someone who's come across concrete evidence that supports that belief. So far they've been willing to go slowly."

Adair held up a hand. "Okay. So we may, on top of everything else, be dealing with a professional thief who is very focused on finding Eleanor's dowry. Today's break-in seems a bit ham-handed for a patient treasure hunter or superthief."

Cam spread his hands. "This break-in today may be the work of someone else."

"We're back to Nathan MacDonald."

"And the man he was arguing with. Or maybe both of them," Cam said.

Adair closed her eyes. "In other words, we're probably dealing with multiple treasure hunters."

"What do we do?" Vi asked.

"We go on doing business as usual. The two of you have a wedding to prepare for. I'm going to dig through the stuff I brought back from the library in Glen Loch and see if I can find what might have convinced someone that the sapphires are still here somewhere on the estate. But what we're all going to do is be very careful. With one of the earrings already discovered, our thief may lose his patience and get desperate."

"You're trying to scare us," Adair said.

Cam glanced from Vi to Adair. "I want you to take precautions. From now on, no one goes anywhere alone—not into town, not down to the lake, not even for a walk. And we all shut the terrace doors whenever we leave a room. I'll work in the main parlor this afternoon."

"You don't think you're being a little paranoid?" Adair asked.

"Humor me," Cam said. "I'm the one who thought Angus One's secret cupboard wasn't a safe hiding place for the earring. You and Vi focus on the wedding," Cam said. "Let me worry about the rest."

"Okay." But she was already worried about the rest. Because "the rest" for her included him.

One thing at a time, she reminded herself as she left the room. Mentally she made her list as she climbed the stairs. Shower first. That would clear her head and help her to think. Then she'd check in with Rexie. That had been on her To Do list earlier, hadn't it?

She thought of the papers that she'd gathered up and crammed into her desk drawer.

So she'd just make another list. And as far as dealing with what had happened between Cam and her, the only thing she was absolutely sure of was that she wanted it to happen again.

10

It was nearly two o'clock when Adair finished the sandwich Vi had brought to her office. The stinging spray of the shower hadn't helped her to clear her head. Or get Cam out of it. Instead, all she'd been able to think of was what had happened at Tinker's Falls. That breathless, heart-stopping jump off the ledge. And what had followed. Especially what had followed.

Just thinking about it had her heart thundering again. Cam had made her fantasy come to life. That little realization hadn't fully struck her until the shower water had turned cold.

Why did that terrify her and thrill her at the same time?

And Cam was not all she should be thinking about right now. But between Bunny and Vi, all the details of the wedding were under control. Caterers, florists, photographers, arrival times. She had a chart on her wall detailing everything. Of course, she and Vi would supervise the setup in the morning. But for now all she had to worry about was the possibility of a runaway bride.

And Cam. Pulling a mini legal pad out of her desk, she tore off three sheets and lined them up in a neat row.

The way she saw it, she faced three major problems:

the Cam Problem, the Missing Sapphires Problem and the Maitland/Banes Wedding Problem. With a pen she labeled each of the papers.

Then she frowned, annoyed that the first problem that had popped into her mind was Cam. In a quick movement she picked that page up and put it in third position. Where it belonged.

Because she wasn't sure she wanted to solve it?

Nonsense. As far back as her memory took her, she had always taken care of herself. She had faced and solved problems all of her life. Practical ones, emotional ones, important ones, trivial ones. They all had to be dealt with by mapping out plans and making decisions. Okay, she'd made a bad one when she'd trusted Bax.

So she'd learn from her mistakes. The trick would be to avoid doing anything rash. She flashed back to that wild plunge she'd taken with Cam off the ledge. Just thinking about it had her heart taking a tumble. But he'd been the rash one. He'd taken the decision right out of her hands— lifting her and stepping out into space.

This time when her heart tumbled, she pressed a fist against it. But what had happened after that, what had happened in the cave—well, she'd been a willing participant in that.

And so what if it had been rash? A girl was entitled to do something outrageous once in her life. Or twice. Or—

Adair lifted the piece of paper with Cam's name on it and turned it facedown on the desk. This was not the problem that she needed to focus her attention on right now.

Neither were Eleanor's sapphires. Cam seemed to have his attention totally focused on solving that one.

She flicked a glance at the French doors that led into the main parlor. Sheer curtains covered the glass squares on the doors, and when she'd passed by them earlier she'd spotted him in silhouette standing at the foot of the portrait, studying it.

When he'd talked about the treasure hunter with the single-minded focus, he might have been describing himself. The sapphires were the real reason he'd come here and if the rest of Eleanor's jewels were still here on the castle grounds, he'd find them. Then he'd go back to his life of adventure with the CIA.

Turning the sapphire paper over, she focused her attention on the problem that deserved her undivided attention. The Maitland/Banes wedding.

Like it or not, the possibility of calling Barry Carlson had been on her To Do list earlier, spurred by the fact that she'd envisioned someone other than Lawrence Banes beneath the stone arch. Someone who looked a lot more like Rexie's first husband than her intended second. Sure, it could have been a figment of her imagination.

But could she depend on that? What if the stones were trying to tell her something?

Right. And why didn't they come and just cart her off to Looney Tunes-ville right now?

She tapped her pen on the paper. What would the harm be if she gave Barry Carlson a call? If Barry turned out to be the cad that Rexie had described, then she'd have some solid information to use in case the bride got cold feet and went into another meltdown.

Opening the desk drawer, she pulled out the jumble of papers she'd crammed into it when she and Cam had first returned to the house. The To Do list had the number of the Carlson Horse Farm on it. Methodically sorting colors into compartments, she slipped everything back into the metal box, placing the larger folded sheets of paper that contained the fantasies on top.

No To Do list.

Pushing back her chair, she dropped to her knees and glanced under her desk.

Nothing.

Crawling around the corner, she peered into the wastebasket. Nary a scrap of paper greeted her inspection.

She was still on her hands and knees, scanning the rest of her office floor for the elusive list, when she heard someone knock on the terrace doors. Starting, she saw an expensive pair of Italian loafers first. Then she took her gaze on a swift journey up perfectly creased trousers and a pristine white shirt. She breathed a sigh of relief when she recognized Lawrence Banes.

Jumping to her feet, she moved forward and hurriedly opened the doors. "Mr. Banes, what a surprise."

And she had a feeling from the expression on his face that it was not going to be a good one.

AN HOUR OF poring over the materials he'd taken from the Glen Loch library convinced Cam that he'd run up against a solid brick wall. Leaning back in the carved oak chair, he planted his feet on the desk in the main parlor. He'd come across an article in the *Glen Loch Gazette* that featured pictures of Angus's secret cupboard, open and shut. But nothing he'd looked at shed any light on the current whereabouts of the rest of the sapphires. They'd been part of Eleanor Campbell MacPherson's dowry, and the only evidence of their existence other than the painting was the earring that Vi and Adair had discovered yesterday.

He'd left a message on his mother's cell but he didn't kid himself that her response would be timely. She and A.D. were taking a working vacation in Scotland, and one of the things that his mother and his stepfather shared was an ability to tune out the rest of the world when they were working. A.D. was painting landscapes for a gallery show and she was doing research for her next historical novel, which would feature the Campbell clan that Angus One had stolen Eleanor away from.

It was a long shot but his mother might have some insights on Eleanor's dowry based on the new research she was doing, and when one of them called back he could fill A.D. in on the security situation.

In the meantime he wasn't any closer to dealing with his other problem—Adair. The curtained French doors that separated the main parlor from her office had allowed him to surreptitiously check on her, more times than he was comfortable with over the past hour. All he knew for certain was that he wanted to make love to her again.

The low rumble of a male voice had him rising and moving quietly to one side of the French doors. She hadn't said she was expecting anyone. With two fingers he pushed against the edge of one of the curtains. The man seated in one of Adair's client chairs had his back to the French doors. He had dark, neatly trimmed hair and the hint of gray told Cam that he was probably somewhere in his forties. Adair's smile was easy and bright but there was a tension in her shoulders. Not fear, he decided. Nerves.

He twisted the knob, eased the door open a crack, then leaned back against the wall to listen.

"I'M SORRY IF I startled you, Ms. MacPherson, but I wanted to see you privately."

Adair's mind raced as she tried to ignore the knot of nerves in her stomach. Even in casual clothes Lawrence Banes looked as if he'd just stepped off the pages of *GQ*. "You've made a long drive for a private conversation."

"Not at all. At Bunny's request I stayed in town overnight at one of the bed-and-breakfasts. She wanted me to be close by because of Rexie. We were all worried about her. But it turned out my help wasn't needed after all. In fact, we decided that a mother-daughter evening was just what Rexie needed to soothe her nerves."

He propped one loafered foot on his knee just as his cell phone vibrated. He slipped it out of his pocket, frowned, then set it on the edge of her desk. Finally he glanced up and smiled at her.

It was the first time that Lawrence Banes had turned the full strength of his charm on her and Adair realized why Rexie might find this man attractive.

"When they left my office two hours ago the wedding was definitely on. Didn't they tell you?"

"Yes. Bunny sent me a text, so I left Glen Loch shortly after they did to keep a business appointment in Albany. About an hour ago Bunny called me back. She told me that Rexie talked to you about her first husband and it evidently stirred up memories."

Adair took a moment to study him. The last person she'd expected to walk into her office unannounced was Lawrence Banes. And in spite of the smile and the casual attitude he was trying to project, there was a tension in him. Albany was a good forty-five-minute drive from the castle, and nothing he'd said so far seemed to warrant him circling back out of his way before returning to Long Island.

"Is that what you wanted to talk to me about?"

"Yes. Bunny and I feel that it's a mistake to remind Rexie of her first marriage, especially when she's feeling so fragile. How much did she tell you about it?" Lawrence asked.

"Not a lot. She told me she and Barry met at Cornell and it was love at first sight. But they came from very different backgrounds." That was about as bare bones as she could make it. Adair hoped that Lawrence would fill in some blanks.

"Different *worlds* is the best way to describe what they came from," he said. "Rexie has led a very pampered life. Her parents have always provided everything for her."

"And you believe you can offer her that same kind of life, the one her parents want for her," Adair said.

"Exactly. Her first husband wanted her to give up everything and go back to live with him in the wilds of Montana. Can you picture that? Anyone can see she doesn't have that kind of strength."

"When did you and Rexie meet?" Adair asked.

"Eight months ago. It was at a charity event the Maitlands were throwing on their estate. Several of my clients were there and they'd offered to introduce me to Bunny and Win. When I first saw Rexie she looked so lonely. Her husband had gone back to Montana for a funeral and stayed. At her mother's suggestion I offered her a sympathetic ear."

"There's quite an age difference between you."

Banes's smile turned wry. "Why is a difference in age always remarked upon? The fact that I'm a bit older than Rexie is probably why I was able to help her get through a bad time."

Banes's phone vibrated. With a slight frown he picked it up. "I have to take this." Rising, he moved quickly to step out onto the terrace.

CAM MOVED AS close as he could get to the doors that opened from the main parlor to the terrace that adjoined the one outside Adair's office. He'd already guessed that the man who'd dropped in on her unannounced was Lawrence Banes and very probably Gianni Scalzo.

He watched Banes walk to the far end of the terrace before he took the call on his cell.

Whatever he said into the phone was muffled by distance. Cam stepped onto the terrace and, using potted trees for cover, edged as close as he could before he dropped down to his knees behind one of them. Luckily Banes was facing in the other direction. If the man turned his way the plant might not offer enough of a shield.

"...told you...I had to talk to her," Banes said.

Cam couldn't make out what the person on the other side of the call was saying. But he could catch the tone. Anger. And he had a lot to say. Cam counted ten good beats before Banes cut the person off.

"I'm going to marry Rexie Maitland." Banes's voice was soft but there was anger there, too.

Banes paced to the far end of the terrace, out of earshot. When he reached the low wall of stones he propped one foot on the top of a flat rock and rested his forearm on his knee.

The stance had recognition streaming through Cam. He was looking at one of the men who'd been at the pond earlier. He would have bet good money on it.

Moving slowly, he began to inch his way back toward the doors to the parlor so that he could be in position when Banes returned to the office.

ADAIR WATCHED THROUGH the open terrace doors as Lawrence Banes lifted his foot to rest it on one of the flat stones bordering the terrace. The instant he placed his forearm on his thigh, his stance and the tension in his body triggered the blurred image that she recalled seeing earlier through that tiny gap in the waterfall. The longer she looked, the more convinced she became that the man she'd seen talking to Nathan MacDonald by the pond had been Lawrence Banes.

How were the two men connected? And why had they been in the woods?

When Lawrence took his foot down, she backed away toward her desk. Shooting a quick glance at the French doors that connected to the main parlor, she was almost sure she saw the shadow of someone through the curtains. So Cam was eavesdropping.

"Sorry about that, Ms. MacPherson." Banes returned to his chair and placed his cell phone on the edge of her desk. He ran a hand through his hair. His smile seemed a bit thinner, his face more tired. "What were we saying?"

"Rexie says that you and her father are involved in some kind of business merger and that the marriage is connected to that," Adair said.

Banes's eyes narrowed. "Win and I are going to sign a partnership agreement right after the ceremony. It's not a secret, but I'm not sure exactly why you've brought it up."

"You seem to be concerned about what Rexie and I talked about this morning. She told me that the deal between you and her father is one of the reasons she's determined to go forward with the wedding."

"Ah," Banes said, relaxing a little. "That sounds like Rexie. She always wants to please her parents. Which is why I wonder how she ever got herself mixed up with the Montana cowboy. But—" Banes raised his hands and spread his fingers "—you know how women are...."

"I do." Adair managed to keep her smile sweet. "But Rexie's first marriage, a mistake or not, was for love. And neither she nor you has mentioned love as one of the reasons for your upcoming marriage."

"Of course I love her," Banes said, his tone a bit hurt. "I was under the impression she loved me. I knew she had concerns about marrying again so soon, and when she read about this place and insisted on having the wedding here I championed her cause. I knew the legend would set her mind at rest."

Adair said nothing.

"I'd expect that you'd be grateful for that, that you'd want this wedding tomorrow just as much as I do. You have a lot riding on it."

"I do." She kept her voice pleasant. "I'm the last person in the world who wants Rexie to call off the wedding. What I don't understand is what you want me to do that I haven't already done."

Lawrence Banes drew in a deep breath and seemed to collect himself. "Sorry. It's just that this wedding means a lot to me. Rexie means a lot to me. Bunny's call upset me because I don't think it's good for Rexie to be thinking about her first marriage. You have no idea how long it took to get her past the divorce papers. She's in a very fragile state. Moving on is the best thing that can happen to her. Once the wedding takes place everything will be fine—for all of us."

In spite of her growing doubts about that, Adair kept her smile bright. "I want you to know that I'm going to do everything possible to make sure that the wedding goes very smoothly on Saturday."

"Good."

As Adair rose, Banes unfolded himself from his chair and glanced at his watch. "I have a pressing appointment. But now that we understand each other, I'm going to leave the matter entirely in your hands."

Adair waited only until Lawrence Banes exited out onto the terrace doors before she circled her desk to follow him. She was only halfway there when Cam stepped into the room.

"I'm almost positive that my nervous about-to-be bride-groom was one of the men we saw at the pond," she said in a low tone.

He smiled at her. "You've got good eyes. And I'm in total agreement."

"But what was he doing there?"

"Very good question. I could go after him and ask him."

Adair saw the reckless gleam flash into his eyes. "Or?"

"We could follow him and see who his pressing appointment is with. Knowledge is power."

"Much better idea. Give me time to tell Aunt Vi."

11

It took Adair three minutes to give Aunt Vi the condensed version of what had happened while Cam alerted Wes Pinter, who was still trimming hedges, that they were leaving. Cam was behind the wheel of his sporty black convertible with the motor running when she slipped into the passenger seat.

"Buckle up," he said. But he didn't wait for her to finish the task before he sent the car flying forward. She clicked the belt in place and clutched the edge of the seat as he floored the gas pedal. By the time they reached the end of the drive and hit the graveled road that twisted away from the castle, the speedometer read fifty and rising.

"Banes has quite a head start," she managed to say as they squealed around the first curve.

"Maybe not so much. Wes Pinter says my car has been the only one parked in the drive since your Mr. MacDonald left."

"So Banes didn't park near the castle, and he lost some time walking to his—" She broke off to suck in a breath as he twisted the car sharply into the next curve.

When the road straightened again he shot her a grin. "Hopefully he has an ego car with less maneuverability."

"Ego car?"

"You know, a sleek, dark colored sedan that shouts, 'I'm successful,' and sucks on a curve like this one."

As he negotiated the next curve, Adair's heart was racing almost as fast as the engine.

"You're good at this," she said.

"CIA training."

As the road leveled for a stretch, she managed to take her eyes away from it and she fastened her attention on Cam. His hands were so sure on the wheel, just as sure and competent as they'd been on her. And he was grinning. She should be scared out of her mind but she wanted to grin, too. "Is this why you went into the CIA? For the excitement? The car chases?" she asked.

"Partly. I love my mom and my brothers, but they're so different. Duncan and my mom are addicted to burying themselves in books and research, although Duncan does get out in the field when his team is working a case. In fact, right now he's in Montana on a big case—tracking a serial killer. Reid loves the straight and narrow. He's totally focused on climbing to the top rung of his job at the Secret Service. I like the variety of the CIA and the fact that I don't always have to follow the rules."

She'd known that Cam was someone who wouldn't be bound by rules the first time she'd ever looked into those twilight-blue eyes. She'd always been attracted to that part of him. Even though she liked rules, relied on them and believed there had to be a reward for following them.

As they crested the hill and shot down the other side, gravel spewed and pinged. Adair held tight and laughed as Cam twisted the car around the next curve. To hell with the rules.

"I eavesdropped on your conversation with Banes. Do

you believe he's marrying Rexie for love or money?" he asked.

She thought for a few seconds. "Yesterday I would have said his motives were strictly business. He was so detached at the rehearsal. He seemed more interested in talking on his cell phone than he was in what was going on. But then he stayed in town last night. And he came to see me today. Maybe he has some feelings for her."

"His cell was keeping him pretty busy while he was talking with you today."

They'd reached the bottom of the hill. Ahead of them the road threaded this way and that before climbing again. Adair spotted a car, a sleek, dark sedan, nearly at the top of the next crest. She pointed a finger. "Looks like an ego car to me."

"Hold on," Cam warned as he floored the gas pedal again.

"The only thing that I'm absolutely sure about is that Lawrence Banes definitely wants to marry Rexie tomorrow. And he doesn't want me to contact the first husband. I had calling Barry Carlson as a possibility on my To Do list, and I couldn't find it when I sorted through the papers I stuffed in that drawer."

"You think Banes might have been in your office before his trip to the pond and saw it?" Cam tapped the brake as he eased into a tricky hairpin curve.

"I'm thinking he took it. And he was worried enough about the possibility of my calling Montana to come back to caution me against it."

"His visit with you didn't go down well with whoever he was talking to on his cell. I couldn't hear everything but Banes did mention that the wedding was on, and the guy on the other end didn't seem pleased. And he and MacDonald were definitely arguing at the falls."

Cam had decreased the speed in order to maneuver through the twists and turns as they climbed the next hill.

"I wish I had a pad and paper so I could draw a time-line," Adair mused aloud.

"Just picture it in your mind as you talk it through," Cam said. "That's what I do."

"Banes says he stayed overnight in Glen Loch to be on call if Bunny needed him. But she didn't. Then this morning he claims he went to Albany for a business meeting and doubled back when she called and told him that Rexie had spoken to me about her first husband. Nathan Mac-Donald also says he was passing through Glen Loch and heard about Castle MacPherson from the locals."

"We can ask Sheriff Skinner to check it out," Cam said. "Be nice if someone saw them together. Be even nicer if Banes is on his way to meet MacDonald right now." Easing the car around the last of the curves Cam pressed his foot harder on the gas.

"Is it too big a leap to think that one of them might have stirred Alba up when Aunt Vi and I unwrapped the earring yesterday?"

Cam grinned at her. "Theorizing possibilities is a key part of an agent's job. Go with it."

"I'm favoring MacDonald. He had that camera with him and it has a telephoto lens. Maybe he was just hiking along the trail that winds through the hills above the castle gardens and he happened to see Alba dig up the earring. Next morning he calls for an appointment and arrives in time to see me racing up to the house with that metal box clutched in my hands."

"He sees it on your desk, then leaves and waits for you to take off for a walk," Cam said. "It's not long after that I follow you and he can walk right into your office and into the main parlor."

"Maybe he calls Banes to join him. Maybe Banes shows up on his own. But they don't find the earring or the rest of the jewels, so they follow us into the woods," Adair said.

"And they have an argument. They leave, but Banes comes back. And whoever contacted him on his cell was not happy about that."

"Then we've got the interesting fact that Banes didn't park his ego car at the castle. Who was he hiding from?" Adair asked.

"Good question. You've got the mind of a good operative."

"Yeah, well, maybe it will be my fallback career if the Banes/Maitland wedding suddenly crashes and burns."

Cam took one hand off the wheel to give hers a quick squeeze. "One thing my CIA trainer always told me—it's not over until the fat lady sings.'"

They were nearly at the top of the hill when the noise erupted, a squeal of tires, then the crash of metal and glass, once, twice, then a final time. The silence afterward was almost louder than the sounds that preceded it.

They crested the hill, and at first they saw nothing. Cam floored the gas pedal and they were halfway down before he spotted the first signs of the skid. Easing his foot onto the brake, he followed the marks around a sharp curve. To their right a fender lay against the trunk of a thick pine.

"Over there," Adair pointed.

Cam braked and pulled to a stop. To the left the land dipped into a gully. Another fender lay close to the road but the sedan had left a trail of crushed saplings in its wake before plowing nearly head-on into a third pine tree.

"Stay here and call for help," Cam ordered as he climbed out and ran toward the sedan.

Adair had already punched in 911 and was talking to

an operator when she reached the side of the road. Cam was pulling the driver's door open.

"He's alive," he shouted up to her. "Unconscious."

As she relayed the information to the 911 operator, Cam dropped to his knees and leaned into the car. She reached him just as he got to his feet.

"I told you to stay put." He gripped her arm to steer her away from the car. But she caught a good glimpse of Lawrence Banes's face. Its pallor had her stomach lurching.

"You're sure he's alive?"

Cam slid his hand down to hers and linked their fingers. "His pulse is steady. He'll be fine. But tell the operator one of his legs may be broken. I don't want to move him. Ask them how long before they can get someone here."

The simple list of orders helped her to breathe again and to focus. When she'd passed along the information, she said, "The EMTs who are on call at Huntleigh College are on their way. Their ETA is less than ten minutes."

"Hey, Sutherland, is this your work?"

Adair whirled around to see a man move away from a large black SUV and start down the hill toward them. He was tall with tanned skin and liberal hints of silver threaded through his jet-black hair. Dark glasses hid his eyes and added a hint of danger to his sharply sculpted features.

Any apprehension she might have been feeling was completely erased when Cam met him halfway up the hill and hugged him warmly. "I got your text earlier but I have to say, your timing is excellent. There's someone I want you to take a look at."

Cam led the way down the incline. "I want you to meet Adair. This is my boss, Daryl Garnett," Cam said.

Adair studied the two men as they reached her. Though

she guessed Garnett was old enough to be Cam's father, they looked more like brothers.

Daryl caught her hand between both of his. "Cam has spoken enough about you that I would have been able to pick a beauty like you out of a crowd."

Adair found herself returning the smile. It seemed to be her day for running into male charm, and Daryl Garnett had a very potent brand.

Daryl glanced over at the car. "Did Sutherland here run this unfortunate man off the road?"

"No," Adair said. "We were just following him."

Daryl glanced at Cam. "Why?"

"We think he might have been involved in a little break-in at the castle, and we were interested in who he might be meeting," Adair said. "He didn't even know we were following him. And we were still quite a ways behind. So Cam isn't to blame for this. Banes must have lost control on that hairpin curve."

"Banes?" Daryl asked.

Cam gestured toward the open car door. "Meet Lawrence Banes. He's supposed to get married at the castle tomorrow."

"Is he dead or alive?" Daryl moved to the open car door.

"Alive," Cam said. "Ambulance is on the way."

Adair began to get a bad feeling as she watched Daryl check for a pulse and then continue to study the man.

"You recognize him," Cam said.

Daryl gestured them to follow him away from the vehicle before he answered Cam's question. "Yeah. It's Scalzo all right."

"Scalzo?" Adair asked.

Daryl glanced back at the car. "And if you didn't facilitate his accident, I'm wondering if someone else did. Wait here."

Adair might have followed Daryl back to the car if Cam hadn't put a hand on her arm. "Who is Scalzo?" she asked again as they watched Daryl drop to the ground and wiggle his way beneath the back end of the car.

"What's he doing?" Adair asked.

"Checking to see what may have caused the skid," Cam said.

"Got an answer there," Daryl grunted as he eased himself out from beneath the car and got to his feet. A second later he joined them. "Someone cut your Mr. Banes's brake lines."

As Adair shifted her gaze from Daryl to Lawrence Banes, her stomach plummeted. "Someone tried to kill my bridegroom?"

"That would be my guess," Daryl said as he pulled out a handkerchief and wiped grease and dirt off his hands.

"Why?" Adair asked.

"It could be that someone recognized him as Gianni Scalzo or one of the other names he's used, or they figured out the investment scam he's currently running and got to him before I did."

"What scam?" Adair asked, glaring at both of them. "And who is Gianni Scalzo? This time one of you better answer me."

Daryl nodded at Cam. "Go ahead."

As Cam told her about his boss's experience with Gianni Scalzo, Adair's stomach plummeted even further. A lightning strike was bad. This was definitely worse. There was no telling how seriously Lawrence Banes was injured, but as soon as he recovered the CIA wanted to put him behind bars.

How many ways could a wedding go wrong?

"I learned today that right after the wedding ceremony the father of the bride, Winston Maitland, is going to transfer millions into Banes's so far very lucrative real estate investments," Daryl added.

"What's wrong with that?" Adair asked.

"Nothing, if the real estate exists somewhere besides on paper. But Scalzo's specialty is running Ponzi schemes and they're only lucrative for a certain length of time. Then the investors lose a lot of money."

A siren sounded in the distance.

"I'm sorry," Cam said. "I couldn't tell you until I had confirmation. There was a chance he wasn't Scalzo."

She raised a hand. "I get it. You're CIA. You specialize in covert, sneaky ops."

Cam winced. "You can deck me if you want."

"Why? Any way you look at it, the wedding is history. There's an injured bridegroom. The CIA is waiting to arrest him. And someone else wants him dead."

There was a moan from the car.

"The two of you go on." Daryl backed away. "I don't want him to see me quite yet."

Adair reached the car first. Lawrence Banes's eyes were open and filled with pain.

"Ms. MacPherson?" he said in a breathy voice. "What—"

She took one of his hands in hers. "Don't try to talk. You've had an accident."

"The wedding..." He broke off, wincing.

"Don't worry about that now," Adair said. On the road above, an ambulance pulled to a stop. "The EMTs are here."

As the young medics rushed down the incline, Banes's eyes drifted shut but his grip on her hand tightened. "Call Bunny. Tell her...wedding is on. I'm marrying Rexie tomorrow."

Stunned, Adair walked back to Daryl with Cam. "He still wants to go through with the wedding."

"Perfect," Daryl said.

"Perfect?" Adair stared at him. "Someone wants to kill him. You want to put him in jail."

"I have a plan," Daryl said. "How would you like to be part of an undercover op?"

12

"I DON'T LIKE IT." Sheriff Morris Skinner made the announcement after Cam and Daryl had taken turns with Adair in filling him in on what had been going on at the castle, up to and including Lawrence Banes's—or more accurately Gianni Scalzo's—car accident.

What the sheriff specifically didn't like was Daryl's plan—the one he'd outlined while the EMTs were transferring the bridegroom to the ambulance. Adair wasn't sure she liked it either since it involved letting the wedding go on as scheduled.

Learning the truth about Lawrence Banes had hit her like a Mack truck, and for the past hour she'd felt as if she'd been sitting on the sidelines watching the men handle everything.

The waiting room in the clinic at Huntleigh College was barely bigger than a walk-in closet, and once Sheriff Skinner had joined them the space had been filled to capacity. The upside of the cramped quarters was that it offered them privacy, and only a soundproof glass wall separated them from the area where Lawrence Banes was being examined and diagnosed by Dr. Barnhill, a young woman in her early thirties who ran a tight ship.

She'd made one appearance in the waiting room to inform them that her patient was suffering from a broken leg and she'd know more about his condition after they'd taken some X-rays. The only thing that she was certain about was that he was determined to get married the next day.

That had been Daryl's cue to explain his let-the-wedding-go-on scenario to Sheriff Skinner.

Skinner pinched the bridge of his nose and sighed. "You're telling me that this Banes/Scalzo guy is an international crook, but I shouldn't arrest him until after he gets married up at the castle tomorrow."

"Correct," Daryl said.

Adair had already played the nightmare scene in her mind. Several times. The setting was the ballroom of the castle with guests looking on. As Lawrence Banes signed the papers with Maitland Investments, law enforcement agencies—some in helicopters, others in black SWAT outfits—would all swoop in to make the arrest of the century.

And each time Rexie Maitland would collapse in tears.

The scene made her head spin so much she couldn't come up with a coherent argument to counter Daryl Garnett's plan. Her groom-not-to-be had created Ponzi schemes across the globe and robbed thousands of people of their savings. The Maitlands and their friends and clients were only the current focus of his business schemes. But if the deal went through on Saturday Banes would be caught. And both she and the sheriff were being asked to be good little soldiers and hold off on letting anyone know until the knot was tied and the papers were signed.

Skinner, a wiry man in his early sixties, set down his notebook and scratched his head. "I've been sheriff here for thirty years, and I've never seen anything like this." He looked at Garnett first. "You say the Portland P.D. has this guy's fingerprints when he was operating under a different alias. Can't they arrest him and take him into custody?"

"Sure," Daryl said. "But the fraud he perpetrated there was twelve years ago. Lots of things can happen in a trial, especially when twelve years have passed. But if we catch him in the act, we've got him."

"I'd like to question him," Skinner said.

"So would I," Daryl agreed amiably. "But that could spook him. The man can disappear faster than the kind of ink they sell in kids' magic kits."

Skinner frowned. "I get that. But I'd like to know who cut his brake lines."

"I've been thinking about that," Daryl said. "Scalzo has always worked with a partner—a man many suspect is the real brains behind their cons. It could be they've had a falling-out. And it would be a real coup if we could catch him, too."

Skinner turned to Adair. "I'd also like to know how one or both of them is connected to the other stuff you think is going on up at the castle. A little trespassing aside, I've never known there to be trouble up there." He shifted his gaze to Cam. "You think someone's been breaking into the castle on a regular basis for the past six months. Could that be Scalzo or this MacDonald character?"

"Scalzo has a social schedule to keep on Long Island," Cam said. "All we know for sure about MacDonald is he seemed interested in Eleanor's missing jewels and he had a run-in with Scalzo at Tinker's Falls."

"Maybe he's Scalzo's elusive partner," Adair said.

Cam exchanged a look with Daryl. "It's a possibility."

"Maybe Banes can help us out there," Skinner said.

"It would be better all around if we didn't question him about his connection to MacDonald," Daryl said. "He doesn't know that Cam and Adair saw them talking in the woods. Better to leave those questions until after the wedding and the arrest."

Skinner encompassed all three of them with his gaze. "I'll talk to Edie who runs the diner in town. She's the best investigator I've got. Everyone goes in there and everyone talks. Maybe she can dig up a connection between the two men that isn't merely theory. In the meantime, I'm going to ask Mr. Lawrence Banes is if he knows who might have cut his brake lines."

Cam exchanged a look with Daryl, then nodded. "Be good if he had a nominee. But Adair here should talk to him first. To firm up plans about the wedding."

As if she were responding to a cue, the young doctor appeared in the waiting room doorway. "Mr. Banes is a lucky man. The fracture was clean. He'll be in a cast for a while, but his tibia will heal nicely. He won't be walking down the aisle or dancing, but he should be able to make the big wedding tomorrow. He's groggy from pain meds." Dr. Barnhill held up a finger. "I'll allow one visitor before he gets his MRI."

Adair rose and followed the doctor into the examining room. The distance was short, but she felt as if she were walking the last mile.

Look at the bright side, Adair. Obviously Lawrence and Rexie were not meant to be. Thank heavens the lightning strike had prevented the young woman from ever kissing the scumbag during the rehearsal. And going along with Daryl's plan would put a very bad man in jail.

What she couldn't quite get out of her mind was what the whole thing was going to do to Rexie. The young woman didn't deserve this. Adair had some idea of what it was like to be dumped unceremoniously by a man. But she was finding it hard to get her mind around what it might be like to discover your second husband was a world-class criminal.

And she couldn't seem to come up with a plan that would give Rexie a second chance at happiness. Formulating solutions, solving problems—those were supposed to be her strong points.

Stepping closer to the bed, Adair studied the man lying there. His eyes were closed and he looked older to her than he had before. She reached out and took his hand. "Mr. Banes?"

His eyes fluttered open, but they looked glazed.

"It's Adair MacPherson."

"Mac...Pherson?" He struggled to focus. "Nurse took my cell. Have to call Bunny. Explain."

When his lids fluttered shut, Adair's stomach knotted. Call Bunny? Why did he want to call Bunny? Why didn't he want to call Rexie?

His eyes opened again and he gripped her hand almost as hard as he had in the car. "You call Bunny. The...wedding. Still on."

"I'll call."

Two technicians in lab coats appeared in the doorway.

"Mr. Banes has to have his MRI now," Dr. Barnhill said.

When she tried to disengage her hand, his eyes opened, and this time they were clear. "Let Bunny know."

She waited as the two young men loaded him onto a gurney.

Bunny? And not one mention of Rexie. Well, Rexie was the person she was going to call. And then she was going to make the phone call that she'd had on her To Do list that morning.

Instead of turning right toward the waiting room, Adair

detoured into the ladies' room. She found Rexie's number on her cell and made the call.

The fourth ring transferred to voice mail. "Sorry, I'm unavailable. Please leave a message after the tone."

Adair disconnected, then frowned. She didn't want to leave this message on voice mail. And it wasn't Rexie whose voice she'd just heard. She could have sworn it was Bunny's voice. Did she have the wrong number?

After checking, she dialed again. Once more it was Bunny's voice apologizing on the voice mail message. Why hadn't she noticed that before? Had she ever called Rexie directly before or had it always been Rexie calling her?

With a shrug, she checked Bunny's number and tried it.

Rexie's mother answered immediately. "Ms. MacPherson, don't tell me there's a problem."

Good afternoon to you, too. "I'm calling for Mr. Banes."

"Lawrence? Then he's talked to you about not upsetting our Rexie again."

"Yes, but he asked me to call on a different matter. He's been in a little fender bender with his car. He has a broken leg, but he's going to be fine. And he wanted me to tell you that the wedding will definitely happen on schedule."

"He's broken his leg?" Bunny's voce was laced with panic and concern. "I want to talk to him."

"I think the doctor has confiscated his cell until he's a bit more coherent. I just saw him and he asked me to call you specifically. But I'd really like to get in touch with Rexie. Since I've actually seen Lawrence and talked to him—"

"I'll tell Rexie. I can handle her, Ms. MacPherson. Talking to her about her first husband just reopened old wounds. I don't want my daughter hurt again. So you need to devote your full attention to making sure this wedding takes place on schedule, and I'll take care of my daughter." Bunny disconnected.

Adair stared down at her phone. Why were both Lawrence and Bunny so concerned that she'd talked to Rexie about Barry Carlson?

A knock sounded on the ladies' room door. "You all right, Adair?"

Cam. "Fine. I'll be right out." She waited until his footsteps faded before she got the number of the Carlson Horse Farm from Information and punched in the number.

After four rings, a female voice came on. "Dr. Carlson is busy with the animals. Please leave a message and he'll get back to you."

"This is Adair MacPherson. It's really important that Dr. Carlson call me. It's about his former wife, Rexie Maitland. The matter is urgent." Then she left her cell number.

It certainly couldn't hurt to find out why in the world Bunny and Lawrence Banes were so upset that she'd talked to Rexie about Barry. Turning, she faced herself in the bathroom mirror.

"In the meantime, there has to be something you can do about the wedding fiasco tomorrow. Think."

WHEN ADAIR JOINED the three men in the small waiting room Cam could feel the change in her energy level. He'd been worried about her ever since Daryl had revealed Banes's real identity to her. She had to be feeling that the sky was falling on her head, and the hell of it was, he hadn't been able to cushion the blow. Nor had he been able to come up with a better scenario than Daryl's.

But she had. He could sense it even before she spoke. "Mr. Banes wants nothing to stand in the way of the wedding. But I've decided that I do."

Daryl stared at her. "I thought you agreed that we need to catch this guy."

"I do. But he doesn't even want to talk to his bride-to-be. He just wants to talk to his mother-in-law-to-be. To make sure she gets her daughter to the wedding. And I don't want Rexie to have two failed marriages on her hands."

"Ms. MacPherson, the man you know as Banes—"

Daryl broke off when Cam put a hand on his arm. "She's got a plan, Daryl. Wait for it. Go ahead, Adair."

"There's no reason why the wedding has to be real, right? All we have to do is convince Banes it's real. We're going to run our own scam."

"I think I'm going to like this," Cam said.

She beamed him a smile before turning to the sheriff. "You can handle it with Reverend Foley, can't you? He can get sick, send in a sub at the last minute?"

"Someone who has no legal authority to marry them." Skinner's eyes sparkled. "I think I might be able to arrange that." Then the sheriff shifted his gaze to Daryl. "With that one modification, I'll agree to go along with your plan."

Daryl raised his two hands in a mock surrender. "I've got no problem with running a scam on a scam artist."

Skinner nodded. "After I interview Banes about his accident I'll post a discreet guard on him here at the clinic. My deputy Timmy can pass for a college student. He also has some technological skills. I'll see if he can plant a bug in the room. In the meantime, I think the three of you might want to get back up to the castle. If I wanted to have some uninterrupted time to search the place, I might figure staging a little accident like this would be a good way to focus everyone's attention elsewhere."

"I'll follow you back," Daryl said to Cam as they left the clinic.

Once they were pulling out of the parking lot, Adair pulled her cell out of her pocket. After the fifth ring she said, "Aunt Vi?"

Turning to Cam she said, "Aunt Vi's fine, but Alba has disappeared."

13

HEARING THE REAL worry in her aunt's voice, Adair turned her speakerphone on. "Aunt Vi, we're on our way back right now." She glanced at her watch. Nearly four-thirty. She quickly calculated. "We'll be there in five minutes. Cam is listening, too. Tell us what happened."

"Alba started acting strangely shortly after you and Cam left. I was working in the kitchen and she began growling at the terrace doors. I had them locked just as we all agreed. Wes Pinter was working on the hedges that run along the back of the garden and I assumed he was disturbing her. Though he never has before."

"What else, Aunt Vi?"

"I settled her down, but she wouldn't move away from the terrace. About half an hour ago she started barking again and scratching at the glass. So I let her out and she tore off through the garden. I didn't catch sight of her again until I got to the edge of the clearing by the stone arch. She ran right through and then she disappeared into the woods beyond. I chased after her, but I slipped and fell on some loose stones on the floor of the arch."

"Are you hurt?" Adair asked.

"No. But stumbling slowed me down. By the time I

reached the trees there was no sign of her. She'd started growling again and I heard a yelp. But I can't even hear her bell now."

"Where are you now, Vi?" Cam asked.

"I'm at the stone arch. There's no one here now. I think Alba chased them away and they may have hurt her."

"Where's Wes Pinter?" Cam asked.

"I can't see him anywhere. I tried him on his cell before Adair called. He didn't pick up."

"Stay right where you are and keep your phone line open," Cam said. "We're only minutes away."

Adair gripped the armrest with all of her might as Cam careened the car onto the dirt road that wound its way through the hills to the castle.

"Aunt Vi?" Pushing down hard on fear, she turned to Cam. "She's not answering. I think I've lost her."

"Almost there," Cam said.

In the rearview mirror she could see Daryl Garnett's car through a cloud of dust. Both men could drive like the devil, but she wished they could go even faster.

"We never should have left her there alone," she said, finally giving voice to the guilt that was plaguing her.

"She isn't alone. Pinter is there. Plus, your aunt's a smart woman."

Adair hung on to all those thoughts as Cam shot his car over the crest of the hill that ended in the castle driveway. Wes Pinter's truck was parked close to the castle. Cam pulled in behind it, and the instant the tires screeched to a halt she jumped out of the car and circled the hood. She could just see the stone arch, nearly a football field away. Pines grew thick and tall on the hill that rose sharply behind it. She started toward them. "Aunt Vi?"

Cam grabbed her arm. "Wait." Then he turned to Daryl,

who'd parked behind them and was already approaching. Quickly he filled him in on their conversation with Vi.

By the time he finished, Vi had appeared from the back of the arch and was running toward them. Adair raced to meet her.

"They make a pretty picture," Daryl murmured to Cam as the two women embraced. Then he strode forward, his hand extended to Vi. "I'm Daryl Garnett, ma'am. I work at the CIA with Cam."

"Viola MacPherson," Vi said as she took his hand.

"Where was the dog the last time you saw her?" Daryl asked.

"She was running into the woods behind the stone arch. That was ten minutes ago. I haven't heard anything since." Vi's hand was still clasped in Daryl's when she turned to Cam and Adair. "I'm worried about Wes Pinter, too. Right after I talked to Adair, I tried to reach him on his cell phone again. I thought he could help me look for Alba. But he didn't answer."

"Why don't we split up?" Daryl suggested. "Ms. MacPherson and I will look for Alba and you two can check on your gardener."

"Sure." Then Cam watched his boss and Vi start back toward the stone arch.

"He sure works fast," Cam murmured.

Adair stared at him. Then she shifted her gaze to Daryl and Vi. "You think he likes Aunt Vi? They just met."

Cam met her eyes. "Sometimes it happens just that fast." That was how it had happened to him. One long look beneath that stone arch and he hadn't recovered since. He couldn't quite get his footing even now. He caught one of her hands and raised it to his lips. "Some of us are just slower realizing it."

The quick flash of understanding and panic he saw in

her eyes was such a perfect match to what he was feeling that it steadied him. He grinned at her. "We have some time to make up for. But first, we have to find Wes Pinter."

Keeping her hand in his, he strode through the garden toward the terrace at the back of the castle. The place was silent except for the noise of their footsteps on the path. But there was no sign of Pinter, nor was there any sound except for the lap of water against the shore below them and the hum of bees. The terrace was empty too and the sinking sun slanted long shadows across the pavers. Nothing looked out of place.

"It's too quiet," Adair said, echoing his thoughts.

The sliders to the kitchen stood open, but the door that led to the rest of the castle was closed. Cam moved toward it.

"Aunt Vi said whoever Alba was barking at was outside," Adair said.

"I just want to check the library." The door was only a short distance down the hall. He still believed that somehow the library held the key they needed. Once he opened the door he said, "Stay close, and see if you notice anything that's been disturbed since we were here earlier."

They walked together down the narrow room, stopping to check the chair near the fireplace where Vi had been sure someone had been sitting quite recently.

"It all looks the same," Adair said.

"Yeah." But he drew her with him all the way to the sliding glass doors that opened onto another terrace. They were locked.

Outside a hummingbird hovered at a bright red feeder, but it shot away like a bullet as soon as Cam opened the door. There was no view of the lake on this side of the castle; instead, paving stones bordered with green moss separated the castle from a well-tended lawn before the treed hillside sloped sharply upward.

Tucked into one corner of the space was a gardening shed, its door slightly ajar. Adair's sharp intake of breath told him that she spotted the boots through the open door just as he did. They broke into a run and found Wes Pinter seated on the floor and rubbing the side of his head.

Cam squatted down. "You all right?"

"Headache. Came back here to put away the hedge trimmers and he sneaked up on me. He slammed the door into me and I must have hit my head pretty good when I fell."

The hazel eyes that met Cam's were undilated and clear.

"I got a look at him," Pinter said. "Shorter than me. Had a mustache and a beard. Longish hair."

Cam glanced at Adair.

"Sounds like MacDonald," she said.

"Is Vi all right?" Pinter asked.

"She's fine." Cam's cell phone rang. After a few seconds, he turned to Adair. "Alba's fine, too. They found her halfway up the hill. Daryl says she was knocked out, as well."

FIFTEEN MINUTES LATER, Cam leaned his hip against a counter while the others sat at the table sipping tea. Wes had fully recovered. And Alba, who sat on Daryl's lap being fed scones, looked as if she was also back to normal.

Not only that, she'd gotten a piece of the bastard who'd hit her. Daryl and Vi had found a good-sized piece of khaki cloth clamped in her jaw, and it had a trace of blood on it.

Wes's description matched with MacDonald, but what had the man been after? Whatever it had been, he hadn't bothered to look in the library for it.

"There are a couple of ways to upgrade the security system here," Daryl was saying to Vi and Adair. "I've no doubt that Cam has several suggestions in mind."

"I do, but I don't think this guy wanted to break into the house today," Cam said.

Adair turned first to look at him. "Why not?"

"He took the time to take out Wes." He turned to Vi. "And you were in the kitchen from the time we left until you let Alba loose, right?"

She nodded.

"He could have seen that. You and the dog were safely inside. Wes wasn't. That's why he knocked him out."

"And Alba found him in the stone arch," Adair said, rising from the table. "That's what he was interested in."

"And he didn't want to be interrupted," Cam said. "I'll check it out. The rest of you stay here with Daryl."

"Not so fast. I'm coming with you," Adair said. "You're the one who made the rule that nobody goes anywhere alone."

"You need any backup, you've got my number on your speed dial," Daryl called after them.

Cam was silent as they walked through the garden to the stone arch. Annoyed, Adair guessed. She'd sensed it in the kitchen while they'd been talking. His jaw was set, his body tense. More than annoyance. He was worried, too.

"Whoever whacked Wes and Alba is long gone," she said.

He glanced up at the hills that rose around them on all sides. Clouds were rolling in fast over the lake, darkening the sky. "He's watching right now. I'd put good money on it. And my instinct tells me that he's getting desperate. He or she didn't foresee that the earring would be discovered in the stone arch."

"I've been wondering about that, too. And why just the one earring? Why split up the pair?"

They'd reached the arch, and Cam glanced up at it. "Maybe the rest of the jewels are here, too. That's what I'd be thinking. I should have taken more precautions with you and your aunt."

"You can't seriously be blaming yourself."

He faced her then. "I was supposed to come up here and keep you and Vi safe. Instead I talked you into chasing after Banes, and that allowed MacDonald or whoever he is to attack an old man and a dog. If we hadn't gotten back here when we did…"

Not just annoyance and worry. There was anger in his eyes and even in the hushed tone of his voice.

Anger at himself.

Her first impulse was to argue with him that she and Vi were perfectly capable of taking care of themselves. But she had a hunch that little lecture would fall on deaf ears. So she tried another approach.

"So now you're rehashing all the should-haves and could-haves. Crying over spilt milk. Is that what they teach you in the CIA?"

He frowned at her. "Of course not."

"Then don't. When one plan fails, what you have to do is concentrate on the next one. That's what I've always done."

Cam stared at her then. "That could be it. If he's the guy who's been visiting the library, he must have been certain that something in there would pinpoint the location of the jewels. Now that he knows where one of the earrings turned up, he's switching to Plan B. You're a genius."

"I am?"

"Bet on it." He pulled her close and gave her a quick kiss. At least she sensed that was his intention. But the moment their mouths met, everything changed. It was as if she'd been struck by lightning.

She felt the heat first, primal, powerful, raw. Then the shock of an electric sizzle shot through her system and thrust her heartbeat into overdrive. Greed followed and it was enormous.

There were other sensations, too—the scrape of his teeth, the thrusting movement of his tongue, the press of those hard hands as they gripped her waist and lifted her to pull her closer.

Each separate, staggering thrill built layer by layer on the earlier ones until she felt as if the pleasure might shatter her. Shatter them both.

Cam couldn't breathe. But there wasn't time to worry about it. He needed more of her.

Her taste consumed him. The variety and uniqueness of her flavors flooded his system until she was once again all he knew. The suspicion lurked in the back of his mind that he might search the world, and no other woman would please him this way or suit him so well.

When she wrapped her arms and legs around him, he wanted more. Needed more. He took two staggering steps forward, pressed her against the wall. And reality came back in an icy rush.

He lifted his head, drew in a breath. "Dammit."

He pried her loose from him, and she sank down on the ledge of rock that ran along one side of the arch. He slapped one hand on the wall to steady himself. Because he couldn't feel his knees. Even then it took him a moment to fully focus. "We need to see what that bastard was doing in here. Figure out his Plan B."

Saying the words aloud helped him focus. He'd lost himself in her. The shocker was that once he'd pressed his mouth to hers he'd been powerless to do otherwise.

Even more terrifying was the fact that he wanted to lose himself in her again. He shifted his gaze away. He'd come here to find what the guy was doing in the stone arch. "Vi said she slipped on some loose stones, right?"

"Yes."

Thunder rolled overhead and he noticed that the sky had gone very dark.

When she made a movement to rise, he said, "You're going to stay here. Right where I can see you and you can see me."

"I know every inch of the inside of this arch."

"Then you can tell me if I'm missing anything."

Pulling out a penlight, he snapped it on. "Stay right here." Then he began to make his way along one side of the wall. One thing he was sure of. However dangerous the threat that the intruder posed, Adair MacPherson posed an even bigger one for him.

Adair watched him move away. She didn't intend to stay put. The feeling would return to her legs any second and she would catch up with him. In the dim backwash of light, she could make out Cam's shadow hugging the wall, his head ducking now and then because of the uneven way the stones arched. He was thorough, running his hand down to the floor and testing for any loose stones.

Closing her eyes, she thought of those hands and the way they could make her feel. And she wanted them on her again. She wanted his mouth on hers again. The first drops of rain splattered loudly on the stones overhead, and the sound had her eyes snapping open.

Her heart took a long fall and then bounced when the realization struck her.

She'd just kissed Cam Sutherland beneath the stone arch.

*No! That wasn't supposed to happen. A fantasy fling
was one thing. Anything else was...*

Lightning flickered and thunder rolled again.

Impossible. Absolutely impossible....

She pressed a hand to her heart and felt a surge of relief that it was beating in the right place. Then she took a
deep breath and reached for calm. It was just the fantasy
that was coming true, she lectured herself. What better
proof did she need than the kiss they'd just exchanged? It
was...better than anything she could have imagined. The
true stuff of fantasies.

And their purpose in being here was not related to her
fantasy or the legend. They had a problem.

She jumped to her feet. "Find anything?"

"Nothing loose or out of place on this side." He started
back to her, using the light to sweep the opposite wall as
he moved.

He hadn't taken more than a few steps when she heard
the crunch of stones beneath his shoes and watched him
squat down.

She rushed to his side. "You found something."

"What part of 'stay there' didn't you understand?"

"I'm with a CIA agent, right?" She was already on
her knees, running her hands along the base of the wall.
"There are some bigger ones loose. Maybe he found another part of Eleanor's dowry."

Cam moved his penlight along the lower part of the
arch. One larger stone jutted out. "Looks like he replaced
some of the stones."

She met his eyes. "No reason to do that if what he
found was the rest of Eleanor's dowry. Unless he wanted
to hide something."

"Our minds are running along the same path."

Before he could stop her, she ducked low and worked

a small rock out of the wall. Then she began to work on the larger one.

Cam grabbed her wrists. "My turn. We don't know what we're going to find."

But she had a feeling it wouldn't be good as she backed up and let him shoot the light into the space she'd cleared. He freed another stone, then handed her the light. "Hold it steady."

Fear shot ice up her spine at what he pulled out next. It was small, no bigger than the metal box she and her sisters had buried their dreams and fantasies in. But it was encased in plastic and there were wires that connected two small canisters.

She swallowed hard. "Definitely not Eleanor's missing dowry."

He met her eyes. "You've got good nerves. This is a type of bomb I've worked on before. Military issue. That's good news. It means he's not cooking up homemade stuff in his cellar."

"Great."

"More good news—there are no other loose stones. I checked. He only had the time to plant one. And there's nothing ticking, no lights blinking. Otherwise we'd both be running like hell."

"I notice you're not doing a happy dance. What's the bad news?"

"This little puppy works on a remote detonator. All our guy has to do is press a button. But even that's good news."

"In what alternate universe?" she asked.

Cam's laugh was soft, and the smile remained on his face when he met her eyes. "I never know what you're going to say next. But the fact that he's using a bomb with a detonator probably means that all he wanted to do today was plant it so that he can set it off later."

"So what are our options?" She was voting for running.

"Make sure he can't set it off. Ever. I'm going to need your help. You game?"

"Sure." He certainly was. In fact, she was pretty sure he was having fun. The look he shot her was cocky, confident. And totally Cam. Her heart fluttered.

"Hold the light steady."

She was surprised that she could, that her hand didn't tremble. His certainly didn't. She watched fascinated while thunder rumbled and rain pounded steadily on the stones overhead. His movements were as deft and quick as a surgeon's as he isolated wires and then used the blade of a small professional-looking penknife to cut them.

When he started to slip the bomb back into place, she said, "Why are you leaving it here?"

"He's got eyes on this place. I don't want him to suspect that we found it."

"He's bound to suspect something if he decides to use that detonator."

Cam met her eyes then. "Then he'll have to try again. And we'll be ready for him."

She stared back down at the device. She knew that the danger was just beginning to sink in when her hand started to tremble. "What did he hope to accomplish with a bomb?"

"I'm thinking maybe it was his Plan B and that it was born out of desperation. The earring was found in here. He's not the only one who's going to speculate that the rest of the dowry is hidden somewhere in the stones."

"Even if he did manage to blow up the whole place, it could take days to sort through the rubble. He's got to be crazy."

"That's one possibility." He finessed the last stone into place. "Our mission is accomplished."

Adair drew in a deep breath and let it out. "What do we do next?"

Thunder roared and lightning flashed brightly enough that for a moment she could see him quite clearly.

"Let Daryl and Vi know. Notify Sheriff Skinner so that he can get someone up here to stake out this part of the garden starting tonight. Then we wait."

"That's it?"

Cam met her eyes. "I know your affection for detailed plans, but aren't you ever tempted to just go with the flow?"

Only with you, she realized. They were kneeling together on the smooth rocks that formed the floor of the arch. Even in the dim light that radiated from the penlight she'd set aside, he looked triumphant, like some warrior that had just won a battle. And she wanted him more than she'd ever wanted anything. Anyone.

And she'd just kissed him under the stone arch.

Panic streaked its way through desire. The kiss didn't matter, she told herself again. It couldn't matter. If any two people were mismatched, it was Cam and her.

Which was why he made the perfect fantasy. That's what fantasies were about. The impossible. The things you think can only happen in your wildest dreams. But she and Cam *were* happening.

"I do like plans. And missions. Right now I have another one for you." Carefully, she set the flashlight down. "We won't need this." Then she tugged his T-shirt out of his jeans. "You won't need your clothes either."

"Sounds like my favorite kind of mission."

He helped her pull the shirt over his head. Even in the shadows she saw the excitement in his eyes darken to something else, something that had fire racing along her nerve endings. But when he lowered his head, she angled hers, avoiding his lips at the last moment.

"No kissing yet. Once we start that, my brain turns to toast." She gave his ear a quick nip. "I want to touch you first."

"Touch away."

She ran her hands over his shoulders, then slowly down his chest. There was so much to absorb—the smooth taut skin, the hard muscle beneath. Even the tickle of hair under her palms sent a separate thrill rippling through her.

"I can't seem to stop wanting you," she murmured as he moved her hands lower.

"It's a mutual problem."

His breath hitched when she slipped her fingers beneath the waistband of his jeans. Their fingers collided, then tangled as they worked on his belt. When it was finally freed, she pushed his hands away.

"My turn. I'll let you know when it's yours."

The sound of his jeans unsnapping seemed as loud as the rumble of thunder overhead. And the rasp of the zipper as she eased it down was exciting, erotic and irresistibly enticing.

"There was no time for me to do this in the cave."

"We were busy with other things. Let me have my turn and—"

The sentence broke off as she slipped her hands beneath his briefs, found him and freed him.

Their gasps intermingled, then thunder rumbled again.

"Oh, my," she breathed. Her experience wasn't vast, but what she was looking at went beyond anything she'd imagined. She ran her fingers up the length of him and felt the tremor move through him. "When you have toast for brains, you miss things."

"There are other things you're missing. Right now. Say the word."

"Not quite yet." The huskiness of his voice had added one more thrill to the mix as she wrapped her fingers around him. When he groaned, power sang through her bringing fresh pleasure.

"I have a plan," she murmured.

"It better not take long."

With a soft laugh, she met his eyes. Then before she could lose her resolve, she leaned in and gave his ear a quick nip, then licked the pain away with her tongue. "I just want to taste you. Try it. You might like it."

Cam wondered if he had a choice. Ever since she'd closed her hand around him, he'd lost all the strength in his arms. By the time she'd used her teeth on his shoulder and moved lower to take his nipple into her mouth, he was sure he was losing his mind. Each flick of her tongue, each scrape of her teeth, each flutter of her breath on his skin created sensations so sharp, so intense they took his breath away. Her mouth left a trail of heat that seemed to sear away his flesh right to the bone.

And all the time, she moved her hand gently on his shaft, up and then down. Up and then down, guiding him into a rhythm that she controlled.

Then she was finally where he wanted her to be, but he still wasn't prepared for what he felt when she flicked her tongue over the head of his penis. The intensity of the pleasure was so great, so consuming. And the ache that it left in its wake was something he'd never experienced.

The only thing he could seem to move was his eyelids. So he watched her as she used her tongue on him. Moving lower to the base of his shaft and then up again as if she were devouring some delicious treat that she'd been starving for.

New sensations battered his system. Agonizing. Amazing. When she took him fully into her mouth, he thought his heart would simply burst out of his chest. No other woman had ever aroused him like this. Seduced him like this. Destroyed him like this.

The power was hers. His entire world had seemed to narrow to the wet heat of her mouth as it drew him in, then released him. And each time she did, he felt parts of himself melting and merging with her.

He wanted it to stop. He wanted it to go on.

Adair was drowning in him. How could she have known that a man's skin could have so many textures, so many flavors? Or that making a man tremble, making him moan, could be so arousing? So amazing? She'd never imagined that she had this kind of power, the kind that brought only pleasure.

Nor could she have imagined her own greed. She couldn't get enough of the taste of him. The textures fascinated her, steel wrapped in velvet. Sensations poured into her, filling all the empty spaces.

When he reached for her, his hands trembled at first, then gripped her and lifted her so that she straddled his thighs.

"Adair." His voice was barely a rasp, but when she started to move, he held her still. "Protection."

Once the word registered in her brain, she met his eyes. "I'm good. Pill. Still my turn."

Then lifting her hips she lowered herself onto him.

The moment she took him in, enclosed him, he began to move. She felt the storm that she'd been building in him since her first touch break free. His thrusts were desperate, violent. This was what she'd wanted. Dreamed of. Then he drove her beyond what she'd ever imagined into a pleasure so dark, so intense that she was blind from it.

"Cam." He was all she knew as he poured himself into her and she shattered.

ADAIR WASN'T SURE how long they lay tangled together against the stones when the ringing of a cell phone forced them back to reality. Cam managed to get to his just as it rang for the third time.

"It's Daryl." Holding it so they both could listen, he said, "Problem?"

"Not on this end. But the storm ended about ten minutes ago, and Vi's beginning to worry about the two of you."

"We're fine now that we've dismantled a very nice military issue bomb."

"No shit," Daryl said. "Sorry I missed it. But Sheriff Skinner called to check on Vi and he's on his way up here. Seems that using Edie at the diner as his investigator has paid off. Hazel Gallinger who runs the General Store caught our friend Banes talking to a stranger on one of her security cameras. Skinner wants to know if the guy is MacDonald."

"Do me a favor and call him back," Cam said. "Tell him we need that extra man he offered to send up here tonight. And tell Vi we're on our way."

14

IT WAS JUST before seven when Sheriff Skinner inserted the security disc from Hazel Gallinger's store into the DVD player in the main parlor. One of his deputies along with Skinner's dog were currently on stakeout duty in the stone arch. Another of the sheriff's men was patrolling the grounds. Daryl and Wes had checked the security system and made sure all the windows and doors were locked.

While they'd provided Skinner with more details on the bomb they'd discovered and the attacks their latest intruder had made, Vi had fixed sandwiches and tea and wheeled the refreshments in on a cart.

In Cam's opinion, they made a pretty motley-looking crew. Skinner looked tired as he pressed a button on the DVD player and then pulled up a ladder-back chair. Daryl had chosen a spot closest to the screen on a love seat next to Vi with Alba snuggled between them.

As the TV screen flickered on, Cam's gaze shifted to Adair who sat cross-legged on the floor. While they'd waited for Sheriff Skinner to arrive, he and Adair had used the excuse of getting caught in the rain to fit in a quick shower and change of clothes.

She wore a T-shirt and jeans and her red hair curled

wildly around her head just the way it had when she was a kid. But she wasn't that kid anymore. Nor was she the young woman who had jarred his hormones into overdrive at his mother's wedding seven years ago.

She was so much more.

He thought of the way she'd held so steady when he'd discovered the bomb. She had courage. He knew that she had to have mixed feelings about letting the wedding go on as scheduled, but he'd studied her face when Daryl had spoken about the hundreds of people that Banes had stolen from over the years. And she'd agreed to the plan even though it might put her dream of establishing the reputation of Castle MacPherson as a prime wedding destination in grave jeopardy.

She wasn't anything he'd expected or even thought he wanted. All he'd known was that she would be different for him. What he hadn't counted on was how different. Or that she would take him so far beyond his expectations—or even his fantasies.

He wanted—no, he needed more time with her. They hadn't had much yet. He also wanted to make love with her again. And he had a feeling that he wasn't going to stop wanting that anytime soon.

When her eyes slid to his, he got that same feeling he'd gotten when they'd been making love—that his whole world was suddenly becoming very narrow. Very centered. The feeling had his stomach skittering and something tightened around his heart.

"This is one of the aisles in Hazel Gallinger's store," Skinner said.

Cam focused on the TV screen.

"She was in Edie's Diner when I came in to ask about any strangers in town. She said she saw two early this morning."

Skinner leaned forward to tap a finger on the screen as a man entered. "She noticed the Banes guy right away because of his fancy shoes and shirt. The next guy came in a few minutes later."

Adair felt the hairs on the back of her neck stand up as the second man entered the store. The screen only showed his back, but he had a camera hanging from a strap over his shoulder. And the hair was the right length for Mac-Donald. She waited, wanting to be sure.

He strolled up the aisle and when Banes turned to him, there was surprise on his face followed by a frown.

"Not a stranger to Banes," she murmured.

"That would be my guess," Skinner said. "And Banes doesn't look happy to see him."

The two men stood face-to-face. It was the shorter man who seemed to be doing all the talking. Then Banes glanced at his watch and nodded. The other man turned away from Banes and the moment he did, Wes Pinter said, "Mustache, fancy beard. That's the guy who attacked me."

"That's also the man who introduced himself to me as Nathan MacDonald." Adair turned to meet Cam's eyes. "And that's the man we saw arguing with Lawrence Banes at Tinker's Falls."

Daryl leaned forward and spoke to the sheriff. "A beard and a mustache, especially one that people remember, is a great disguise. If you'd be willing to lend me that disc, I can get a good enough image off it to send to a tech I know. He'll run it through a facial recognition program minus the beard. Then we might know who we're dealing with." He turned to Cam. "It may match up with that old photo I have of Gianni Scalzo's partner."

Skinner ejected the disc and handed it over. "Banes claims that he has no idea who might have tampered with his brake lines. He's going full steam ahead with the wedding. By the time I left his room, he was pestering Dr. Barnhill for a phone so that he could to talk to Bunny."

Bunny again. Adair frowned and found herself looking at Cam. She wanted to talk to him about the fact that Banes hadn't once mentioned talking to Rexie. Something about that was still rubbing her the wrong way. She wanted his take on it, and she just wanted time to be with him. Everything had happened so fast between them. And time was slipping away. After tomorrow, after he and Daryl and the sheriff were able to arrest Banes, they'd probably have to go back to Washington. She and Vi would have their hands full with the fallout from the wedding disaster.

All her life she'd focused on mapping out plans for her future. No one had ever made her want to live so totally in the moment. In the now.

"I wish we had a better handle on what the hell is going on here," Skinner said.

Adair shifted her focus back to the conversation.

"All we've got are theories or suppositions." Cam stretched his legs out. "If MacDonald is the guy who's been poking around in the castle for the past six months, I'd say his goal is the sapphires. Something must have convinced him that they exist and they're here. Maybe it started out as a hobby. But now he's convinced they're in the stone arch, and he's determined to get them before the hills come alive with other fortune hunters."

"If he's Scalzo's longtime partner and he cut Scalzo's brake lines, the partnership is obviously on the rocks. The question is why?" Daryl said. "And why now? They've been together for years. Why have a falling-out the day before a wedding that promises to net them millions?"

"He could be both our nocturnal visitor and Banes's partner," Adair said. "The Maitlands signed the contract for the wedding about six months ago, the same time Vi started to have her sleep disturbed and brought Alba home. If MacDonald is the man behind the scenes, his job could be intelligence gathering, right?"

"That has always been my assessment," Daryl said. "What are you thinking?"

"Maybe MacDonald decided to take the jewels on as a private project and didn't inform Banes," Adair continued. "Then the earring shows up and Banes gets wind of it and MacDonald doesn't want to share. They argue. MacDonald tries to eliminate Banes."

"Damn good theory," Daryl said.

"Ninety-nine percent of marriages that break up do so because of differences over money. I imagine the same thing could happen to a partnership," Vi said.

"And with this kind of money at stake, it might explain why things are getting so volatile so fast," Skinner said. "Whoever he is, the MacDonald guy is dangerous. And he's had professional training."

"Plus, he's versatile," Daryl said. "He cuts Scalzo's brake lines, takes out Wes here and a dog without leaving permanent damage, and plants a bomb."

"A regular one-man army." Skinner rose from his chair. "Before Wes and I leave I want you to fill me in on the schedule for tomorrow."

"I can take you into my office," Adair said. "The entire day is on the wall."

CAM PACED BACK and forth in his room. They'd done all that they could do for the moment. Daryl had a tech working to identify Nathan MacDonald. Banes was being guarded by Skinner's deputy in the hospital, and two of his other men were working surveillance on both the stone arch and the castle grounds.

He glanced at his watch. It was late—well past midnight. Adair had a full day tomorrow. They all did. He should let her get her rest. He should get some of his own.

Moving to the sliding doors that led to the balcony, he stepped outside. The storm had cleared and a full moon bathed the garden below him. He could even see the outline of the stone arch. As he watched, two figures stepped off the garden path and started across the clearing toward the stones. He recognized them immediately. Daryl and Vi. When they reached the shelter of the arch, he saw Daryl take Vi into his arms.

His boss clearly wasn't wasting any time.

And hadn't he already wasted enough? For seven years he'd avoided Adair. And those were years he could never get back.

Turning, he stepped back into his room, locked the slider, then strode to the door of his room and reached for the handle. The thought struck him just as he was about to step into the hallway. He was close to being obsessed with her.

Just as obsessed as Banes was with his wedding and this Nathan MacDonald seemed to be with the sapphires.

How in hell had he let it come to this?

ADAIR LAY ON her back counting sheep. Fifty-seven of them so far. But about every five sheep or so, she lost her focus and started thinking about Cam. And wanting him.

Opening her eyes, she stared up at the ceiling. Twenty-four hours ago he hadn't been a part of her life. She hadn't seen him in seven years. And they'd only made love twice. Surely it took longer than that to develop an addiction.

Yet, as ridiculous as it seemed, she wanted him now—so badly that she couldn't sleep. Sitting up, she twisted around and punched her pillow several times, then lay back down and closed her eyes.

Seven sheep later, her mind drifted right back to Cam as if it were on a magnetic tractor beam.

After the sheriff had left, he'd told her that he was going to work with Daryl for a while and that she should get some sleep. They all had a big day ahead of them.

Rolling over on her back, she stared up at the ceiling. It promised to be a big day all right. A big disastrous day.

She hadn't been able to speak with Rexie yet. Bunny had called to confirm their arrival time for the photograph session, but Rexie was busy with her bachelorette party and couldn't come to the phone.

And Dr. Barry Carlson had yet to call her back. She'd tried him again earlier right before she'd joined everyone in the main parlor for the viewing of Hazel Gallinger's security disc. She'd reached the answering service. Again.

Had Rexie found it that difficult to get in touch with him when he'd originally moved back to Montana?

And then she remembered that she'd wanted to talk to Cam about it. And why shouldn't she? She had a perfectly good excuse to go to his room in the middle of the night—one that didn't mean she was becoming a sex addict.

Throwing the covers back, she leaped out of bed and rushed to the door. Just as she reached it, there was a soft knock, and she threw it open to find Cam.

Grabbing his shirt, she pulled him into the room. "I need to talk to you."

Talk was the furthest thing from Cam's mind once the moonlight poured over her. She was a vision—red curls tumbling over porcelain skin, a shimmer of lace and silk that skimmed her breasts and dropped only to the tops of her thighs. And those eyes, a dark gleam of green. She stopped his breath.

When she nudged him onto the bed, he sat. His legs wouldn't hold him up.

She paced. "Rexie's first husband. I want to get in touch with him."

Cam struggled to focus on what she was saying and found it helped if he fastened his gaze on a point beyond her. "The first husband?"

"Dr. Barry Carlson. He's a vet and they met at Cornell when he was finishing up and she was just starting. It was love at first sight, they got secretly married and then the fact that they came from very different worlds came crashing down on them. The families were not happy. His parents expected him to come back to Montana, and hers pictured her stepping into a well-established social circle on Long Island. They went with her parents' scenario. Not surprising once you've met Bunny."

"The charmer who ran me off the road."

"Exactly. It's such an old story." She waved her hand in an "and so forth" gesture. "But something about the way they broke up keeps nagging at me. It's not like I don't have a big enough worry list. There's a wedding tomorrow that has to go off without a hitch so this Scalzo person can be brought to justice. And there's this Nathan MacDonald still skulking around out there with his martial arts training and his bombs. And there's the rest of Eleanor's dowry. But I can't seem to let Rexie's first marriage go. Does this ever happen to you when you're working on a case?"

"Yeah." She had his attention now. He couldn't help but notice that what was happening between the two of them hadn't made her worry list. And it seemed to be right at the top of his.

She climbed onto the bed near the headboard and

crossed her legs beneath her. "Then maybe you can help me. Tell me I'm wrong."

"First, what bothers you about the breakup?"

"Rexie's still in love with him. I could see it in her eyes. It was the kind of love at first sight that she'll never shake loose. Do you know what I mean?"

Something skittered through Cam's stomach. Ridiculous to think he might know exactly what she was talking about. What he said was, "Classic. Like *Romeo and Juliet* without the feuding families."

"Precisely." She scooched a little closer to him on the mattress. "You may be on to something. If Romeo hadn't killed Juliet's cousin and had to flee the city, how long do you think it would have taken for the Montagues and Capulets to get together and put an end to the marriage?"

"Probably not long. They were blood enemies and they'd each want their child back. They might have been able to handle the friar because his goal all along was to end the feud."

"And the Carlsons and the Maitlands weren't even feuding. In fact they might have had a common goal, a dream for their only child that they wanted to see come to fruition. To fulfill that dream, they needed their child back."

Cam studied her as he thought about the possibility she was suggesting. "You actually think the parents might have had a hand in the breakup?"

"I'm beginning to wonder. Bunny Maitland is a very focused woman. She's got a daughter who in her view has married the wrong man. Then enter from stage right the perfect man for her daughter—Lawrence Banes. Ta da! In Bunny's eyes he's Prince Charming, and in his eyes, Rexie's the ticket to getting a small fortune from Maitland Investments."

"You think Banes was just lucky or did they team up?" Cam asked.

"It may have started out as accidentally serendipitous, but they're certainly working as a team now. When I talked to him right after the accident and then again in the clinic, he wanted me to call Bunny and say that the wedding was definitely on. Bunny, not Rexie. Maybe one of them got the Carlsons on board. I'd put good money on Bunny for that. Think about it. Two mothers with a common goal—they want the happiness of their child. A funeral might have started it all, but it got Dr. Barry to go back there—and then the communication lines break down. Rexie claims he stopped returning her calls. When I try to call either one of them, all I can do is leave a message. And it's Bunny's voice on Rexie's voice mail that tells me to leave it."

"Shades of *Romeo and Juliet* again," Cam mused. "Messages gone astray or intentionally blocked."

"Exactly. I want to fix it," Adair said. "If I could just figure out a way to get Barry and Rexie in the same room together."

He tilted his head to study her. Each time he was with her, he learned something new about her. "This wedding destination thing isn't just business for you. You're a true romantic."

She stared at him, shocked. "No. My sister Nell is the romantic. Piper is the cynic. I'm just plain practical."

But he was beginning to see that beneath the surface, she wasn't. She might work hard at giving off that vibe, but did a practical woman bury her secret goals and sexual fantasies in a stone arch because she believed it to have special powers?

For the first time since he'd come into the room, he took his eyes off her and swept his gaze around the space, noting even in the moonlight the feminine lines of the little love seat tucked away in an alcove and the vase of flowers on a nearby table. And there were candles in various shapes and sizes on a carved cherry dresser and more on the small nightstand.

It wasn't the way he would have imagined her room, but he thought it fit the woman he was coming to know—the woman who'd penned an action-adventure fantasy and buried it in a legendary stone arch.

"I have a plan." Two plans, he thought, as he rose and began to light the tapered candles. One of them would have to wait a bit. The other wouldn't.

"I'd say don't keep me in suspense, but I'm guessing that you're lighting the candles as a part of a plan to seduce me."

"All that covert training wasted." He found her CD player, selected an album and pressed a button. Debussey poured softly into the room. "I hope you won't rat me out to Daryl. He'll have me sent back to the farm for a brushup course."

"My lips are sealed."

"And they're lovely lips," he said as he joined her on the bed again.

Surprise flickered in her eyes. "You don't have to say that."

No, he didn't have to say it. More importantly, he hadn't ever said it before. "Shhh." He leaned forward, brushed his mouth over hers.

Words. He'd found them for other women. Why was he having problems finding them for her? Drawing back, he met her eyes. "Do you remember the day our parents married?"

"Of course, I do."

"You were standing there on one side of the stone arch

with your hand on Reid's arm. Your dress was pale green and your curls…" He reached out to twine one of them around his finger. "They were all tumbled down like they are tonight, and there was a green ribbon the color of your eyes threaded through them."

Adair stared at him. "You remember my hair and what I was wearing?"

"I remember everything about you. I couldn't take my eyes off of you. And then you looked at me. Do you remember?"

All Adair could do was nod.

"My heart stopped."

Hers was stopping now.

He dropped the curl and ran just the tips of his fingers along her jawline. "I wanted you in a way that I'd never wanted any woman before."

The words weakened her so much that she could do nothing but stare at him.

"And I want you even more now."

They sat on the bed, their faces close, their mouths only inches apart. But when he moved, it wasn't to close the distance. Instead he rose and began to take off his shirt.

Without speaking, she got off the bed, as well, and they worked together to take off his clothes. Not too fast this time. The shirt came first, and when her hand encountered that firm warm flesh, she absorbed the first shock of heat. It took them longer to discard the jeans and shoes. But there was more pleasure as she watched the denim move down narrow hips and strong thighs.

When he was naked, he surprised her by lifting her off of her feet and then lowering them both to the bed. "My turn," he murmured. "I want to look and touch."

And he delivered on the words, tracing her face with

his fingers, rubbing her lower lip with his thumb, then trailing it lower to her throat where her pulse beat so fast.

"Your skin is so delicate looking in the candlelight. Like one of the porcelain dolls my mother used to keep locked away in a cabinet. She wouldn't allow my brothers and me to touch them for fear they'd break."

"I won't break."

"I know." He brushed his thumb over her collarbone, then moved his hand down the silk camisole to where it skimmed the tops of her thighs. "I think it's always been the contrasts in you that fascinate me. I thought of touching you like this the day of the wedding. Here." He trailed his fingers down her thigh, then up again and beneath the lacy hem of the nightie.

"Here." He began to trace a lazy pattern over her panties. Layer after layer of pleasure radiated through her from the clever movement of his fingers.

She arched up, trying to get him to the right spot, then went totally limp when he pushed the lace aside and slipped two fingers into her.

Only then did he lower his mouth to hers. As he slowly took the kiss deeper, matching the movements of his lips and tongue to the rhythm of his fingers, Adair felt everything else slip away.

There was only Cam. There was only this incredible pleasure he alone could give her.

As he guided her slowly higher and higher, he felt the surrender. Savored it, wanted to prolong it. But the first thread of his control slipped.

She was his. Knowing that, treasuring that, he had no thought but to give her more. And to take more.

As greed built, as the need to possess grew, his kiss became more demanding. Linking her arms around his neck, she moved with him, demanding more, taking more and more. His pulse pounded in faster and wilder rhythms as she fisted around his fingers. He knew the moment the pleasure grew unbearably tight inside of her, felt her shudder beneath him when it broke free.

Her arms were still around him holding him tight when he raised his head. "Look at me, Adair."

Her eyes, still filled with the pleasure he'd given her, met his.

"My turn again," he said. Then he let control snap.

The soft, dreamy pleasure he'd trapped her in vanished the instant he drove into her. The shock of his fast powerful thrusts, the glory of it had her crying out, wanting more. And he gave her more. Gave them both more.

Aroused. Thrilled. She met the demand, matching his unreasonable speed beat for beat. Her orgasm was fast too, ripping through her, then lingering in little aftershocks, until it erupted again when he reached his own release.

Afterward, when he could think again, Cam found that she was still beneath him, holding him tight. When he shifted to the side so that he wasn't crushing her, she snuggled into him.

"Don't go."

The words were barely a whisper, but they triggered a warmth that spread through him like a slow-moving river. He'd had no intention of leaving her to go back to his own bed, he realized, as he tugged up the covers.

That was a first for him, too. Though he couldn't explain it, watching her fall asleep on his shoulder in the flickering candlelight felt quite simply right. He lay there absorbing the feeling, relishing it, until her breathing had steadied and he was sure she slept. Slipping quietly from the bed, he retrieved his cell phone, then moved out onto the balcony of her room as he punched in his brother Duncan's number.

Duncan picked up after the first ring. "Trouble or a favor?"

Cam laughed softly. "We always call each other for the same reasons, don't we?"

"What are brothers for? Which is it?"

"A favor," Cam said. "If you're still in Montana?"

"Until tomorrow. I'm still fishing, but if you need—"

"The favor I need you for is in Montana." He gave Duncan the short version of the situation at the castle, the wedding problem, and then explained what he had in mind. "Can you do it?"

"It's an extraction operation, right?" Duncan asked. "You want me to go to the Carlson Horse Ranch and bring this Dr. Barry Carlson to Castle MacPherson. Doesn't the CIA usually send in a team to do this kind of thing?"

"It's not a CIA operation. And it has nothing to do with the sapphire earring or the other problems here at the castle. It's personal."

"How soon do you need him?"

"In the morning would be nice. Afternoon would do it. How soon can you get him here?"

Duncan snorted. "If I were Commander of the Starship Enterprise, I could beam him to you in a matter of moments."

Cam didn't reply because he could almost hear the wheels in his brother's head beginning to whir. Although it was the research angle that had drawn his brother to the FBI profiling unit, Duncan was very effective in the field.

"What are you planning?" Cam finally asked.

"I've got the location of the farm. It's about an hour from Billings, hour and a half from where I am. I'll have a couple of scenarios in mind by the time I get there."

"I just bet you will."

"Luckily I still have our team's private jet at my disposal, but you are going to owe me big-time for this."

"Keep me posted," Cam said.

"Ditto."

After disconnecting, Cam quietly slipped back into bed with Adair.

ADAIR HUMMED A little tune in her head as she stepped out of her room into the hallway. It was the first time in her life that she'd ever started the day with lovemaking, the first time she'd ever showered with a man. The first time she'd ever been in love.

That last little item on her mental list had her stumbling down the last step onto the landing above the foyer.

In love? When she felt that little flutter again right under her heart, she pressed a hand hard against her chest. The gesture did nothing to stop the sprint of panic. She was not in love with Cam Sutherland. He was her fantasy fling.

And she could not think about this right now. It didn't help that her gaze was fixed on the foyer where she and Cam had rolled on the floor that first night.

Which was barely a day and a half ago.

Don't think about it.

With her free hand she dragged a list out of her pocket. At nine o'clock Sheriff Skinner was supposed to arrive for an update. By eleven the caterers would arrive. And by one in the afternoon Bunny and Rexie Maitland and the wedding party would be here for photos.

But the first thing she needed was coffee. Taking a sharp right, she hurried down the hallway to the kitchen, then stopped short in the doorway.

Daryl Garnett and her Aunt Vi were locked in an embrace.

Before she could recover enough to make a quick retreat, Daryl drew away. "Adair is here."

Vi turned and beamed a smile at her.

Daryl signaled Alba, who was stretched out near the terrace doors. "I'll take the dog out for a run."

Even after Daryl had shut the sliders behind him, Adair still couldn't think of what to say. And she almost always could.

"I've shocked you," Vi said, a blush rising in her cheeks.

"No." Adair went to her then and took her hands. "You really like him, don't you?"

"Yes. Don't you?"

"Yes." Adair realized that it was true. She'd liked Daryl from the moment he'd walked down that incline and greeted Cam with a hug. "Cam thinks the world of him."

"When I first saw him, he reminded me a bit of Clint Eastwood—the *Dirty Harry* movies—dangerous, competent. He knew just what to do with Alba, finding the bump on her head, checking her eyes."

She turned then to look through the glass doors as Daryl threw a stick. Alba raced off to fetch it. "She loves him now."

It certainly seemed so, Adair thought as the dog raced back to drop the stick at Daryl's feet. He crouched down, and she licked his face lavishly.

"I love him, too," Vi said.

Adair stared at her aunt, uneasiness and happiness making a queasy mix in her stomach. "You're serious."

"Yes." Vi met her eyes and smiled. "It was love at first sight. I thought that only happened in books or movies or for Angus One and Eleanor. But I think I fell in love with Daryl from the moment he took my hand and told Cam that we'd go find Alba."

She drew Adair with her to the table so they could both

sit down. "It makes my knees weak to think about it. And I know exactly what you're going to say."

"You do?" Adair wasn't sure at all.

"You think it's too soon to know for sure and that falling in love and planning a future with someone takes a great deal of thought and a detailed plan."

A future? The queasiness in her stomach intensified. But it wasn't her aunt and Daryl she was worrying about now. How could you possibly plan a future with someone when you never knew what it would bring? Or how soon it might end.

"Aunt Vi, are you sure?"

"I've never been more sure. Oh, it flustered me at first to believe a man could be attracted to me after all these years. And it was a shock to realize that he could make me feel this way—giddy and...beautiful. He makes me feel beautiful, Adair."

Adair squeezed her aunt's hand. "Then I love him, too."

Vi leaned closer and kept her voice low. "I did the riskiest thing last night."

"You made love with him, I hope."

Vi blushed prettily. "Oh, yes. But first I took him out to the stone arch, and I kissed him. I wanted to make absolutely sure that he's it for me."

The women were holding each other and laughing when Cam entered the kitchen.

"Sorry to break this up, but the sheriff just pulled up. I think our strategy session is about to begin."

HALF AN HOUR later, Adair was perfectly clear on one thing. Her first big wedding at Castle MacPherson, as promised, had turned into an undercover op. Daryl had begun their meeting by having everyone coordinate their cell phones so that they could reach each other instantly on speed dial. They also had a code word to use if they needed help. "Angus" meant that there was a problem. "Eleanor" meant they had a full-out code red.

One day she was going to look back on this and laugh. For now she merely refilled her coffee mug. The tea seemed to be equally good. Vi had poured Daryl three cups. Her aunt looked like she was having the time of her life. Her cheeks were flushed, her eyes bright. Even brighter when she looked at Daryl Garnett.

"Essentially," Daryl said, "we've got a groom running a major scam and he has to marry the girl to get the money. And we want him to sign the agreement with Maitland before we arrest him. Otherwise we've got him only on intent to defraud and we'll have to hope that the chain of evidence in Oregon hasn't deteriorated or disappeared. Not to mention that if Scalzo makes bail on those charges, he'll pouf again."

"There's one other little twist we can add to the mix," Skinner said. "My deputy has learned that at Banes's request Bunny Maitland has hired a security service to provide protection for him. They arrived at the clinic late last night and they'll be transporting him to the wedding."

"So he's more worried about the cut brake lines than he wanted to admit to the local sheriff," Daryl said.

"And he may have a pretty good idea of who cut them," Cam said. Then he turned to Adair. "Why don't you take us through the schedule one last time?"

Adair went to the wall chart. Bunny Maitland had taken her over it so many times she could have recited it in her sleep. "The florist and caterers will arrive at eleven and begin setting up the ballroom for the reception. That's in the east wing." She pointed to the large room at the back of the castle.

"The bride and her parents along with the maid of honor

and the flower girl will arrive at one, and they'll use a suite of rooms above the ballroom to dress." She shifted her finger on the floor plan. "The groom and his best man and his new security entourage will arrive at two and they'll use a room over in the west wing. A team of photographers will cover all of that. Guests should start arriving at three-thirty, and the actual saying of the vows will occur at four-thirty, followed by champagne and food and dancing in the ballroom and the cutting of the cake at five-thirty or so."

She turned back to face the others. "If the groom hasn't been arrested by then."

"But the signing of the partnership agreement and any wire transfers that Banes will make—that could take place at any point in any room," Skinner pointed out.

Daryl rose to stand in front of the floor plan. "Maitland has held off on the signing until Scalzo actually marries his daughter. I'm betting that they'll close the deal directly after the ceremony." He tapped a finger on the floor plan. "They could use the groom's suite for privacy. Plus, it's close to the garden and almost on their way to the ballroom."

"Logical," Cam said. "Unless they make the signing part of the official celebration—a sort of welcome-to-the-family thing."

"We should be able to cover either option and pick up Banes as soon as he drives that proverbial nail into his coffin," Skinner said. "I've still got my deputy on him at the clinic. He'll follow Banes and his bodyguards and see that he gets here. But that still leaves us with the problem of this MacDonald guy. His agenda doesn't seem to be as clear."

"I've got an idea about that." Daryl moved back to his chair to pick up the folder he'd been carrying earlier. "I had time to play around with Adair's computer last night. I sent some images to a good tech man and he was able to send me these."

He opened the folder and passed each of them side-by-side enlarged photos of two men. "I had my guy age an old photo I had of Scalzo's partner. Then I had him take the beard and long hair off our friend MacDonald."

For a moment there was complete silence as they all studied the images.

"If it's not the same man, they're related," Skinner said.

The nods in the room testified to everyone's agreement.

"And he and Scalzo have had a falling-out." Cam leaned back in his chair, crossed his legs at the ankles. "Both of them were in the area when the earring was discovered, so both of them could have it on their radar. Which gives MacDonald two reasons to show up at the wedding. One, to finish off Banes, and two, to get the earring."

"If he does show up," Vi said, "Alba will know."

Daryl pulled another set of prints out of his folder. "I've also run off some copies of MacDonald as he appeared in the security disc with the beard. Even though I doubt he'll try to make an appearance in that persona again."

"No," Cam agreed. "He'll choose something that will blend in. That's his M.O."

As Daryl passed the pictures out, he said, "I figure we don't bother the catering and florist people because we don't want to spook the bridal party. But with the sheriff's two men and the four of us, we've still got quite a few people looking for this guy. We all have to blend in, too. This is a small wedding and we can't let Banes suspect that there's a bunch of security people here."

As the rest of them continued to discuss the blending-in part, Cam drew Adair aside. "You're nervous."

"It goes with the job." The concern in his eyes touched

her. "I'd be nervous even if we weren't planning to destroy a bride's wedding, catch a major criminal and try to predict what a crazy man might do."

"We'll all be on the lookout for MacDonald. Skinner's good and Daryl and I aren't half-bad." He leaned down and kissed her nose. "Just focus on doing your job. It's all going to work like clockwork. The wedding will take place, Banes will be arrested and you'll find a way to handle Rexie's heartbreak."

This time Adair felt more than a flutter beneath her heart. As she stood with him while the morning light poured through the terrace doors, she realized that it wasn't Rexie's heartbreak that was worrying her. It was her own.

15

"THEY MAKE A good team," Daryl said.

"I was thinking the same thing." Cam stood with his boss observing the two women through one of the archways that opened into the castle's official ballroom. Alba lay at Daryl's feet while Vi and Adair worked both separately and together to orchestrate an amazing transformation. Two hours ago the room had been an empty expanse of gleaming parquet floors and cream-colored walls. Now linen-covered tables were scattered along the walls to serve as food and drink stations. Flowers were everywhere.

Daryl sent a sidelong glance at Cam. "We're doing everything we can to keep them safe."

Cam knew that. The problem was that no one had so far gotten access to the castle who looked anything like Nathan MacDonald. And they'd been looked at by a lot of people. None of the florists or caterers or any of their drivers bore any resemblance to the images that Daryl's tech man had captured on the prints.

"I promised Vi we wouldn't let anything happen to Adair. So we won't."

No, they wouldn't. Adair was in business mode with

her curls sternly disciplined into a knot at the back of her head. She wore a professional-looking pale gray linen suit. A notebook was in her hand and she kept methodically checking things off.

"I've never met a woman quite like her," Daryl said.

Since the words echoed his own thoughts, it took Cam a beat to realize that Daryl was talking about Vi.

Turning, Cam studied his friend's face. Daryl was looking at Vi as if he simply couldn't take his eyes off of her.

"She was the last thing I was expecting when I came up here," Daryl said. "But she's it for me. She's everything I want."

Cam shifted his gaze back to Adair. She was it for him, too. Hadn't he know that seven years ago when he stood with her under the stones? He turned back to Daryl. "So what are you going to do about it?"

Daryl met his eyes. "I'm going to adjust my plans to include Viola MacPherson. I'm going to ask her to marry me. But first, we have a fake wedding to pull off and an arrest to make."

As if on cue, Cam's cell phone rang. It was Sheriff Skinner. "The bride's side of the wedding party and a photographer have arrived."

"This is where the fun starts," Daryl said.

Two hours later, Adair took the stairs two at a time and ran full tilt into Cam on the landing.

"Whoa," he said. "Stop. Take a breath. Everything's fine in the bride's suite."

She narrowed her eyes. "How do you know?"

"I edged the door open and took a peek. Bunny is running the photo session like a little general."

It would be a waste of time to tell him he wasn't supposed to be peeking. "I need to check in with them anyway. The groom and the best man are here safe and sound in their room. The father of the bride has joined them for coffee."

He smiled at her. "Confess. You sneaked a peek in there, didn't you?"

"I didn't have to. Daryl has the room pretty well staked out. And Aunt Vi just took a tray of sandwiches and some tea and coffee in. The two hired security people are going to get Banes to the stone arch in a wheelchair. The doctor hasn't okayed the crutches yet."

"What did I tell you? Everything is proceeding like clockwork," Cam said. "And I have some good news for you."

"What?"

"After our talk last night, I called my brother Duncan and sent him on what you might call a little fishing expedition."

She narrowed her eyes on him. "And that is good news because?"

"He's in Montana. He paid a visit to the Carlson Horse Farm, and he caught quite a big fish."

She grabbed his arms. "Will you stop talking in CIA code and tell me? What did he find out?"

"Your theory about blocked messages and conspiracy were right. And your hunch that the mothers were engineering that part was spot-on. After Barry went home for the funeral, Bunny and Barry's mother became very friendly. Bunny evidently explained in great detail just how unhappy Barry was in the practice on Long Island and convinced the other woman to help her thwart communication between the two kids. Mrs. Carlson came up with a few creative ideas of her own. Barry wasn't even aware he'd sent Rexie a letter asking for a divorce, nor that he'd signed the divorce agreement. His mother admitted to Duncan that she got his signature both times in a flurry of paperwork she handed him."

"Duncan found all this out since we talked last night?"

"He's a damned good agent. An even better brother. He's bringing the doctor here even as we speak. Barry wants to talk to Rexie. I thought maybe it might help to tell her that when Lawrence gets arrested and hauled away."

Adair grabbed him and kissed him long enough and hard enough to make her head spin. "Thanks." She had to blink to clear her vision. "I'll thank you better later. But I have to get to the bridal suite."

"Everything's going like clockwork," he repeated before he released her.

Adair hurried up the rest of the stairs. The problem was that everything *was* going like clockwork. But that didn't mean squat. Because so far no one had spotted Nathan MacDonald. The only drama that had occurred so far was when Alba started barking her head off at the limo that delivered the bride and her attendants to the front door. After that, Aunt Vi had banished Alba to the kitchen.

She knocked once and then stepped into the suite she'd assigned to Rexie and her bridal party. The photo shoot was in full swing. Bunny had hired a team of photographers. One was assigned to Lawrence Banes, another was taking candids of the arriving guests. And yet another had arrived with Rexie, her attendants and her mother in the limo.

There were flowers here, too, along with the remains of the champagne and sandwich tray she'd sent up right after she'd originally escorted them to the room. She'd had no time to speak privately with Rexie, but the young woman wasn't nearly as nervous as she'd been at the rehearsal.

Not that she looked terribly happy. More determined. But even if she was a tad short of glowing, she made a beautiful bride. The photographer, a woman with straight, chin-length black hair and seriously framed glasses, had Rexie posing in front of a full-length mirror. The maid of honor and the flower girl stood to one side while Bunny peered over the photographer's shoulder.

"Stand up straight, Rexie honey," Bunny directed. Then, stepping to the side of the photographer, she showed the woman a photo. "Make sure you capture the full length of the train in the mirror. Rexie's dress is a copy of the one I wore for my wedding, and I want the picture to look exactly like this one."

"No problem, Mrs. Maitland." The photographer took several shots.

If Rexie was less than glowing, her mother more than made up for it. Adair thought of Rexie's first wedding—an elopement that Bunny had missed. In spite of herself, she felt a tug of sympathy for the woman. And she couldn't deny the amount of work that Bunny was putting in to make sure that this day was perfect—for both of them.

Then Bunny waved the maid of honor and the flower girl into the photo frame. The camera began clicking again.

"Smile, Rexie," Bunny encouraged. "This is the happiest day of your life."

Adair felt her stomach tighten, then ruthlessly ignored the feeling. However bad today was for the poor bride, there were going to be happier days ahead. And one day— soon, she hoped—Rexie would be very grateful that she hadn't actually married Lawrence Banes.

When the photographer paused for a moment, Rexie sent Adair a smile and a wave. Bunny turned around and hurried toward her.

"What's wrong?" she spoke in a low voice as she

reached Adair. "Is it Lawrence? Has something happened?"

"No. He's here. The photographer is taking pictures as we speak. The guests are being directed to parking areas. Everything's moving along right on schedule."

Bunny glanced back at the photo shoot. The glow on her face had faded. "We don't have any shots with the flowers yet. Can you handle that? I have a list of the poses I want."

"Of course."

Bunny handed her the paper. "I need to see Lawrence. I need to know that nothing else unexpected is going to happen."

Adair felt another pang of empathy for the woman. A groom in a leg cast and wheelchair was probably not the way that Bunny had envisioned her daughter's wedding pictures.

And there were worse disappointments to come. She put a hand on Bunny's arm. "It's going to work out." She had to believe that.

"I just want my daughter to be happy. From the time she was a little girl, I've wanted to give her the perfect wedding day."

Adair's heart sank. But she managed to say, "Lawrence wants that, too. And he's here. You have to give him kudos for that."

"Yes. Okay." Bunny drew in a deep breath and let it out. "I still have to check on him. The bouquets are in the adjoining room."

"I'll take care of it." Adair glanced at her watch. Less than a half hour to wedding march time. "When the photographer's finished, I'll bring them all down."

The second she closed the door to the suite behind Bunny, Adair leaned against it and allowed herself one deep breath. The photographer gestured the maid of honor and the flower girl to the side, then shifted to take shots of the bride from a different angle.

"Jennie and I will help you get the bouquets," the maid of honor said.

As Adair followed them, she passed the full-length mirror and she as she did, something in the reflection tugged at her memory. In the doorway of the adjoining room, she glanced back to identify what might have caught her attention.

Nothing.

The photographer had moved to take a different shot. She was a woman in her forties, with a sturdy build and one of those enviably straight, black bobs that no doubt required regular appointments in an expensive salon. And she was good with Rexie, talking softly to her as she raised the camera to take the next shot, then shifting position and lifting the camera again.

Nerves, she thought. And she didn't have time for them now. It wasn't until she lifted the bridal bouquet out of its box that she felt the tug again. And this time she realized what was causing it.

Images flashed into her mind. The photographer's hands, the familiar way they gripped and moved the camera.

Then came the voices. Daryl saying that wigs were standard tools of disguise. Alba barking when the bridal limo had arrived and Vi banishing her to the kitchen. Cam saying that the way best way to get into the wedding would be to "blend in."

Adair shoved down hard on the hysterical laugh that threatened to bubble out. What better way to blend in than to arrive in the bridal limo with the bride and her mother?

Her mind was spinning so fast that she wasn't even

aware she'd moved back into the main room until she heard Rexie's gasp. "Oooooh, they're beautiful."

Jerking her mind back to the present, Adair crossed to the young girl and handed her the cascade of roses and lilies of the valley. The remaining shots had to be taken. And she had to think.

But her mind had switched from fast-forward mode to slow motion. Any small hope she had of being mistaken or hallucinating faded as she watched the photographer take the next series of shots.

She was looking at Nathan MacDonald all right. The hands, even the way he let the camera hang from the strap on his shoulder—it was all so familiar. Why hadn't she noticed it sooner?

There was no time to plan, but she knew what she had to do—she had to separate MacDonald from the bridal party and she had to keep him away. If his goal was to get revenge on Banes by stopping the wedding, Rexie could be in mortal danger. And if his goal was to get the sapphire, well, she could use that as a distraction.

Walking forward, she took Rexie's hands in hers. "It's time to go. Lawrence is already on his way to the stone arch." She barely kept her hands from trembling as she gathered up the train and gave it to the maid of honor. "You're in charge. Once you get to the foyer, go straight out through the front door and then wait on the garden path just as we did at the rehearsal."

Out of the corner of her eye, she watched MacDonald cover his camera lens and move toward his case.

"Aren't you coming with us?" Rexie asked.

"I'll be right behind you. I have a couple of shots to discuss with the photographer. Your mother gave me this list."

Then without another look at MacDonald, she shooed them out of the suite.

IT WAS ALBA'S muffled barking that drew Cam from his post in the foyer to the kitchen. He had to nudge the dog away from the door as he entered.

"What's upsetting her?" he asked Vi as he patted the dog's head.

"She wants to go out that door."

As if to prove the point, Alba moved to it and then turned to stare at them.

"I can't let her out," Vi explained. "Not after the commotion she caused earlier when the bridal party arrived in that limo."

Alba didn't move away from the door. She stood her ground even when Daryl entered through the sliding terrace doors.

"Anything?" Vi asked him.

"Everything's running smoothly outside," Daryl said. "The last of the guests are parking. Both Mr. and Mrs. Maitland joined the groom for the photo shoot, and from what I could hear through the terrace doors they intend to sign the papers there right after the ceremony."

"But so far there's been no sign of Nathan MacDonald," Vi said.

Daryl looked at Cam. "Maybe he's decided to keep a safe distance, wait until Scalzo is in the stone arch, and then detonate the bomb."

"I don't think that's the plan. At least not his whole plan, because it doesn't get him the earring. That's got to be what he's after. Scalzo's partner is a patient man. He works behind the scenes, researching the targets, gathering data. So he's had time since the *Times* article to look into the connection between the missing sapphires and the

Queen of Scots. For fifteen years he's been content to stay out of the limelight. That all fits with the person who's been visiting the library. Then suddenly he comes out of the shadows to pay a personal visit to the castle to talk to Adair. That visit to Adair wasn't about Banes. It was all about the earring. The best chance he has of getting it is through Adair. I'm betting she's his target."

He whirled back to face them. "And he had a camera when she gave him the wedding tour. Maybe that's how he's blending in."

"One of the photographers," Daryl said.

"The last time I saw her she was headed toward the bridal—" The ringing of his cell cut Cam off. He glanced at the caller ID. "It's Adair."

But when he held it to his ear, he heard nothing.

16

ADAIR PAUSED AT the top of the stairs, waiting until the two women and the little girl rounded the landing and started down to the foyer. Only then did she slip her hand into her pocket and close it around her cell.

"Thank you, Ms. MacPherson."

The voice sent a chill down her spine. Because it was Nathan MacDonald's voice. Not the husky voice of the photographer.

"For what?" She kept the smile on her face as she turned to face him. Then for just an instant her mind went blank. It wasn't a camera he held in his hand now, but a small, efficient-looking gun.

"For getting rid of the girls so that we could discuss our business."

"Business?" Slowly Adair drew her gaze away from the weapon and met MacDonald's eyes. The large framed glasses were gone now and she could see that his eyes were calm. And cold. Cold enough to send another chill through her system.

"No need to panic," he assured her. "I just have a proposition for you."

"A proposition? I don't understand." Adair struggled

for composure. He was able to read her too well. And she wasn't going to panic. She couldn't afford to. In her pocket, she pressed the number that she hoped was Cam's and sent the call.

"Oh, I think you do. But we can't talk here." He smiled as he gestured for her to move away from the stairs and away from the bridal suite they'd just left. "We need some place quiet away from the wedding party and guests."

"The library. It's in the west wing. We'll be alone." Adair led the way down the corridor.

"You can stop pretending that you don't recognize me as Nathan MacDonald. I have very good survival instincts. I felt it the moment my disguise failed me. I was sure of it when you rushed the bride and her attendants out of the room. And you saved me the trouble of finding an excuse to keep you behind. After all, the wedding must go on, right?"

Right. Opening the door, she led the way along the balcony that formed the second floor of the library. She heard a muffled sneeze behind her and kept walking to the sliding doors that opened onto the outside balcony. "This was Eleanor's favorite room."

Another muffled sneeze.

She had no idea if her call had gotten through, but she'd remembered the code word—"Eleanor" meant code red. That small detail gave her confidence. Turning, she faced MacDonald and the gun.

"SHIT." SWEARING HELPED hold off the fear. Cam held his cell pressed to his ear, then nearly tripped over Alba as he led the way out of the kitchen.

"Is Adair all right?' Vi asked.

That was the uppermost question in his mind. "I can barely hear her." But he'd caught one muffled word. *El-*

eanor. Code Red. So MacDonald had her. But he didn't want to say it. Couldn't afford to think about it. Not when he had to keep fear and panic at bay.

In the foyer he cursed silently when they had to pause for the bride and the two attendants cascading down the stairs.

"Where's Adair?" Vi asked them.

"She's right behind us with the photographer," Rexie said. "We're supposed to wait for them on the garden path."

Just then Alba began to bark.

"Where is—" Cam turned, searching for the dog.

"Alba stopped at the door to the library," Daryl said.

Of course, Cam thought. It was the logical place for them to go. And Adair's mind was very logical. She'd want him away from the wedding. And for MacDonald, the library had to be the room he was most familiar with. He'd suspect that the key to finding the rest of the jewels would be there. For the next few minutes—he doubted they had more—he had to think the way Adair and the man threatening her would think.

He took Vi's hands. "You take the wedding party outside and go on with the ceremony. I'll send Adair to you as soon as I can."

Vi met his eyes for a minute, then nodded. "I'll hold you to that."

Then she smiled at Rexie and led her away with her attendants.

"The library." He spoke in a low voice to Daryl as they walked back to where Alba was barking. "Alba knows where they are."

"The damn photographer," Daryl said. "The dog tried to tell us when the bridal limo arrived."

When they reached the door, Cam turned to his friend. "Here's what we're going to do."

Less than sixty seconds later, he was climbing up the wall to the right of the library's balcony.

"YOU'RE ALREADY FAMILIAR with the space, aren't you?" Adair asked. "You've been spending a lot of time here."

He glanced around. "No. You left it off my tour the other day." He nearly sneezed, but caught himself in time. His hand remained steady on the gun.

"Let me open the balcony doors and let in some air," she offered. If Cam decided to climb up the outside wall, he'd need access to the room.

MacDonald muffled another sneeze and gestured her to go ahead. She shoved them all the way open. The only sound that drifted in was the breeze ruffling the pines. The wedding hadn't begun yet. But surely someone had to have noticed she was missing. Bunny would. So would Vi. Somehow the message would get to Cam. All she had to do was keep MacDonald talking. "So what exactly is your business proposition?"

"You seem to be a practical person, Ms. MacPherson, so I want to make you a deal. You give me the sapphire earring you found the other day and I'll let you get on with your big wedding. So much depends on it. The future of your fledgling business as well as the little sting operation you're cooperating in."

Adair simply stared at him.

He laughed then, but the sound was threaded with anger, not amusement. "Oh, I know what you're up to. I waited around to see if Lawrence Banes survived his little accident yesterday. And I recognized Daryl Garnett, CIA agent extraordinaire, the moment he got out of his car. I'm not as stupid as my longtime partner. I told him six months ago that it was time to take the money we'd made and run. The Securities and Exchange Commission was sniffing around. They've become more vigilant lately. But he couldn't pass up the extra fortune he could make by marrying Winston Maitland's daughter. The agreement they sign today will allow my partner to access millions with a few strokes of his fingers on a computer keyboard. The money will be in his offshore accounts before the cake is cut. And I taught him everything he knows."

MacDonald's voice had risen steadily, driven by his growing anger. Adair heard Alba start barking above it. The sound was muffled. Distant. The dog would know where they were, but she had to keep MacDonald talking and distracted so that Cam could make his move. "Your partner wouldn't listen to you."

"No."

For the first time, Adair saw the full strength of the man's fury in his eyes. It bordered on madness. And it had to be fueled by more than a disagreement over money. Outside, she heard the music begin. The wedding party had assembled. The fake minister had taken his place.

"But you stood by him and tried to convince him for six months. What did he do to make you want to kill him?"

"He told me that he wanted to buy me out. He'd give me half the money we'd already made and then I could take a hike. My services would no longer be needed."

He used the fingers of his free hand to tap his chest. "*My* services that planned every con we've pulled for over fifteen years. *My* services that had allowed him to escape the law on several occasions and kept him out of jail."

"He dumped you."

"No. I'm going to dump him. I thought of killing him, but it will be much more satisfying to think of him rotting in jail. Especially when he learns that I used his precious wedding as a cover to walk away with a priceless sapphire."

He dipped his free hand into his pocket and pulled out a small black box. "But I'm flexible on that. If you don't give me that earring, I'll press this button and there'll be an explosion in the stone arch. While it's filled with people."

The music changed, signaling that the bridal attendants should line up near the end of the garden path. The groom and his best man had taken their places beneath the stone arch. She could picture it so clearly in her mind. Where was Cam?

"The clock is ticking," MacDonald said with a smile that didn't reach his eyes.

She caught a glimpse of Cam to the right of the balcony door. But MacDonald still had the gun. She had to rattle him enough to allow Cam to make his move.

"The earring," MacDonald prompted. "I was up in the hills after the rehearsal and I saw you and your aunt find it. You know where it is. I researched this place in your local library this morning. The most obvious place to hide it was Angus One's secret cupboard. It wasn't there. But you know where it is."

"Yes, I know exactly where it is." Adair folded her arms over her chest. "Someone told me once that it's not over until the fat lady sings. And I'm not going to give you the earring."

"You have to." Some of the fury in his eyes was replaced by surprise. "You have to or I'll blow everyone up. I'm not kidding."

"No, you're not kidding." She pointed to the device he held in his hand. "But you're not going to be able to pull it off. That thing won't work. We defused the bomb."

"No. You're lying." But he glanced down at the box in his hand. And in that second of inattention, Cam gripped the ledge at the top of the balcony doors and swung his feet through and up to knock the gun out of MacDonald's hand. He landed close enough to plant a fist in the man's face.

MacDonald fell like a rock.

"Good work, Princess," Cam said as he quickly turned the man over and secured his wrists.

"You good up there?" Daryl called.

Adair saw him step out from beneath the balcony, his gun raised.

"Yeah." Then Cam grinned at Adair. "Get out of here. You've got a wedding to run."

It's not over until the fat lady sings.

Adair kept repeating the phrase over and over in her head as she raced down the garden path. She wanted to make sure that when that song finally came, there'd be a happy ending for Rexie. And there was one thing she still had to do.

The wedding march hadn't started yet. She had time. Careening around the last curve, she caught sight of the bridal party just as her aunt Vi signaled the maid of honor to start down the aisle.

"Rexie," she said breathlessly as she reached them. "I need…a word?"

Without waiting for an answer, she took the girl's hands and drew her out of earshot of her father.

The wedding march began.

"What is it?" Rexie asked, her eyes wide.

Adair leaned close enough to whisper. "Don't kiss Lawrence."

Rexie stared at her. "What about the legend? I thought the kissing part was the whole idea."

"Rexie, it's time." Winston's voice was soft, but very firm.

Over Rexie's shoulder, Adair saw that the guests had all turned in their direction.

"Make some excuse. He's in a wheelchair," Adair whispered urgently. "Tell him you'll make it up to him later. I don't have time to explain. Just trust me."

Rexie nodded, then turned to her father and let him lead her away.

All Adair could think of to do now was cross her fingers. When Vi joined her, she filled her aunt in on what had happened in the library. "Cam and Daryl have everything under control." Now all they had to do was get through a fake wedding and the arrest of the groom. "One villain down and one to go."

She tried not to think about the devastated bride.

Vi took one of her hands and squeezed it as Lawrence Banes took Rexie's hand from her father's. "I want to know what you told her before you sent her up the aisle."

"I told her not to kiss Lawrence. The marriage might not be real, but I just couldn't let her kiss him beneath the stones."

Vi chuckled. "That's my girl."

"Except I ran the risk of turning her into a runaway bride."

"She's not running."

As soon as Winston Maitland returned to the first row of chairs to take his seat next to Bunny, the fake minister began, "We are gathered here together..."

Adair hardly dared to breathe until he pronounced them man and wife.

When Rexie gave her new husband a hug instead of a kiss, Adair clapped her hands in relief while the guests applauded their congratulations.

The wedding party was halfway down the aisle of chairs when Cam joined her.

"Good news," he said. "Sheriff Skinner just got a call from his man who was screening the guests as they arrived, and it seems we have some party crashers."

"Duncan and Barry?" she asked.

"I told my brother to keep Dr. Carlson in the car until we get the bridegroom and the father of the bride back into their suite. Daryl and Sheriff Skinner are running that show."

Vi looked from one to the other. "Dr. Carlson—you're talking about Rexie's first husband?"

"Yes," Adair said. "Cam arranged for Duncan to extract him from Montana. Can you distract Bunny for a bit while I talk to Rexie?"

Vi's eyes gleamed. "I know just what to do. I'm sure she'll want to help me lead the guests into the ballroom." She hurried away.

Cam linked his fingers with hers as they watched Winston Maitland and two security men wheel Scalzo off to the groom's suite. Vi was true to her word. She had Bunny's ear. A moment later the two women were headed toward the castle and the guests were following them down the path.

A photographer was posing the bride and her two attendants beneath one of the arbors.

"You got a plan once you get Barry and Rexie together?" Cam asked.

"I don't have a clue," she admitted, and tried very hard to ignore the nerves jittering in her stomach. "Any advice?"

"Do what you're good at. Jump in feetfirst and go with the flow."

That had never been what she thought she was good at, but she didn't have a choice. "I'm going to send the maid of honor and the flower girl to the castle. Then I'll take

Rexie to the stone arch to talk with her. When I give you the signal, you call Duncan and have him deliver Barry. Then can you go and help Aunt Vi keep Bunny and the guests occupied?"

"Will do." He couldn't have come up with a better plan himself, Cam thought as she walked away.

Once she had Rexie alone, she took her hands and drew her toward the stone arch. "There's someone here who wants to talk to you," she said. "But first, I have a story to tell you."

Adair waited until she and Rexie were seated on the ledge that ran along the inside of the stone arch before she told it. "There's bad news and good news," she began.

"You're scaring me," Rexie said.

Adair took both of her hands and related the Lawrence Banes/Gianni Scalzo story, including the fact that he would be arrested any moment and taken to jail. Rexie didn't interrupt, but Adair could read every emotion on her face—disbelief, shock, horror.

"I married a crook."

"No," Adair said. "I told you there was good news. You're not married at all. The man who presided over the ceremony wasn't a minister. He had no authority to marry you. You're still a single woman."

A sheen of tears appeared in Rexie's eyes, but there was relief, too. "Really?"

Adair squeezed her hands. "Really. And I think I might have even better news. There's someone here who wants to talk to you."

"Who?"

Nerves knotted in Adair's stomach. This part could go either way. But she turned and signaled Cam. Seconds later, a man stepped out of one of the parked cars in the driveway and ran toward the stone arch.

Adair stepped a distance away to give the couple privacy. But the look in Rexie's eyes when she'd seen Barry Carlson had told her everything. Hope and love. Those two things were what the legend of the stone arch were built upon. It had been what had worked for Eleanor and Angus One. And when Barry took Rexie into his arms and kissed her, Adair knew exactly what she was going to do next.

In the rose arbor, Cam lingered long enough to see Barry Carlson kiss Rexie Maitland beneath the stones. They would find their happy ever after now.

The question was: would he?

17

CAM WATCHED ADAIR for a moment longer, debating whether or not to join her. He'd told Duncan to hang around and keep an eye on things. And she'd asked him to keep the parents occupied. But first he had to check on how Daryl's sting operation was going down. Not that he doubted for a minute that it would run smoothly.

Turning, he wound his way down the garden path following the last of the guests. The terrace doors to the groom's suite were open. Pausing, he used one of the trees in the garden for cover and looked into the room. Gianni Scalzo sat at a table in front of a laptop. It was running like clockwork, he thought. A couple of strokes on the keyboard and Winston Maitland was offering his new "son-in-law" a cigar. The moment that Daryl and Sheriff Skinner stepped into the room, Cam moved closer so that he had a clear view of Scalzo's face. And the man was good. Even as Skinner read him his rights, Scalzo registered only innocence and confusion. He turned to Maitland. "They're making a mistake. You have to vouch for me. I just made you and your clients very rich. I just married your daughter. I'm family."

Daryl stepped forward with the handcuffs. "You just

tried to fleece him for every penny he's got. And this time we've caught you in the act."

He clamped one of the cuffs to Scalzo's wrists and the other to the arm of the wheelchair. Then he met the man's eyes. "I told you back in Italy we'd meet again."

"You." Scalzo yanked at the cuffs.

"Yeah." Daryl smiled at him. "Payback's a bitch, isn't it?"

"You'll never prove a thing," Scalzo said, his voice rising.

"We've got enough to put you away for a very long time," Daryl said. "But even if we didn't, your ex-partner's going to turn on you just the way you turned on him."

Cam had the very great pleasure of seeing Gianni Scalzo turn pale.

"I don't know what you're talking about."

"You will," Daryl said.

Cam waited until the sheriff and one of his men wheeled Scalzo out before he strode into the room to join Daryl. "You okay?" he asked.

Daryl grinned at him. "It was almost worth the wait to see the look on his face when he realized he's not going to wiggle out of this one."

Cam turned his attention to Maitland then. The man's face was nearly as white as Scalzo's had been. He'd want to be with his wife and daughter. But Adair needed more time. He moved toward him. "Mr. Maitland, why don't you come with Daryl and me?"

A HALF HOUR later, Cam sat with the Maitlands, Vi and Daryl in a small anteroom that offered privacy as well as a view of the ballroom where guests were sipping champagne and enjoying the view of the lake.

Daryl had filled them both in on Lawrence Banes's

real identity and the fact that he'd been discreetly escorted off the grounds by Sheriff Skinner and his men. Then Cam had told them about Barry Carlson's arrival and the bare-bones sketch he'd received from his brother Duncan. Bunny's complexion had paled considerably while he and Daryl were talking.

As Cam wound it up, Maitland turned to his wife. "You actually conspired with Barry's mother to engineer our daughter's divorce? Why?"

"Because I love her." Bunny pulled a handkerchief out of her purse and dabbed at her eyes. "She was so unhappy. And he was trying to convince her to go back to Montana with him. I couldn't let that happen. And then Lawrence came into our circle. He was just perfect. And that's all I ever wanted for Rexie—a perfect wedding day, a perfect marriage."

Maitland shook his head, but he reached for his wife's hand. "The only thing Lawrence Banes was perfect at was running a con."

Eyes sheened with tears, Bunny lifted her head and met her husband's gaze, "You liked him. You were the one who thought up the business merger."

"Maybe not," Daryl said, addressing Maitland. "I'm betting it was one of your clients who introduced you to Banes, and you only brought it up after you heard the buzz about how profitable his investments were."

Maitland frowned as he thought for a moment. "As I recall, it did happen that way."

Cam looked at Bunny. "Was it your idea to get Barry's mother involved?"

It was Bunny's turn to frown. "Lawrence may have suggested it. He was so empathetic to Rexie's unhappiness and my desire to change that. He mentioned that Barry's mother might feel the same way. So I called her and we decided that they'd be happier if they stayed in their own worlds. She just wanted what was best for her son."

"And Banes—did he also suggest that you could help things along if you kept them from talking or communicating with one another?"

"Yes," Bunny admitted. "And it worked."

"Dammit, Bunny. Banes nearly ruined us," Maitland said. "And think what it's going to do to Rexie's happiness when we have to tell her the truth about him."

"He's damn good at what he used to do," Daryl said. "I've been chasing him for over fifteen years."

Bunny glanced through the glass doors at the guests who were now casting curious glances at them. "He certainly ruined my daughter's wedding day."

"Maybe not," Cam said. He'd caught a glimpse of Adair threading her way through the guests with Rexie and Barry in tow.

Once she'd entered the room, she beamed a smile at everyone. "Mr. and Mrs. Maitland, this is a first at Castle MacPherson. Today you are going to get two weddings for the price of one."

It was a double wedding day he would never forget, Cam decided. Two for the price of one is exactly what Adair had delivered. Cam stood with his brother at the edge of the ballroom terrace as Dr. Barry Carlson danced with his bride under the stars. Bunny Maitland was giving instructions to a photographer while Adair stood at the edge of the dance floor waiting to cue the bride's father. The young couple had been remarried beneath the stone arch just as the sun had set on the lake. By a real minister this time.

"Good work, bro," Cam murmured to his brother.

"I'd say it was good work all around." Daryl joined them and passed out beers.

"Compared to the two of you, my extraction mission wasn't much of a challenge," Duncan said. "All I had to do was explain what had evidently been going on to Barry. His mother caved right away and admitted to conspiring with Bunny Maitland. But she'd been having second thoughts for months because her son wasn't happy, and he was still calling Rexie. The truth was he'd been planning a trip back to Long Island to see if she'd at least talk to him in person. I'm really sorry that I didn't get him here in time to help out with the sting operation."

"You did play a role in that," Cam said. "The fact that I was able to let Adair know that you were bringing Carlson back helped her to pull off the fake wedding. And you definitely played a role in getting Barry and Rexie their happy ending."

On the dance floor, Winston Maitland cut in on the groom to dance with his daughter.

"Speaking of our little sting," Daryl said, "I checked in with Sheriff Skinner and he says that MacDonald is still so angry with his old partner that he's singing his head off. Which means that their victims will be getting at least some of their money back. The only thing he won't admit to is breaking into the library. He admits that he knew about the missing sapphires, but never gave them much thought until he saw Adair and Vi unwrap the earring."

Cam frowned. "That means there's still someone out there who has been sneaking into the castle on a regular basis."

"A new higher-tech security system will put an end to that," Duncan said.

"Not if what they're after is the rest of Eleanor's dowry," Cam countered. "And now that one of the pieces has shown up, I'd be more motivated than ever to find the rest."

Duncan sipped his beer. "Since it looks like the two of you will be paying regular visits to the castle, you'll just have to track them down first."

Cam nearly choked on his beer, and Daryl laughed. "We always have room for an FBI profiler. Why don't you join us?"

Duncan raised his free hand, palm outward. "Not me. I'm staying as far away from that stone arch as I can get."

"Good luck with that," Daryl said. "I'm going to dance with my fiancée."

"Fiancée?" Cam murmured as Daryl walked away.

Duncan clapped him on the shoulder. "I had a chat with Vi. Your boss doesn't believe in wasting time."

No, Daryl didn't waste time. A good CIA agent didn't. And Cam felt he'd wasted seven years already. But it was impossible to get Adair alone. The cake had to be cut, the bridal bouquet had to be tossed, an endless number of pictures had to be shot. And everyone wanted to dance with Adair. He'd had to cut in on the groom to get a word with her.

"You worked a miracle today," he murmured as he pressed her close.

"No, the legend did all the work," she said.

"You were the one who talked them into getting re-married here today."

Adair smiled up at him. "I got the idea when they kissed beneath the stone arch. I mean—why not? Their fate was sealed."

Hadn't he thought the same thing when he'd seen them kiss? And his fate was sealed, too. For seven years he'd avoided accepting that.

"We need to talk," he said.

"Sure. Later." She smiled at him as the father of the bride cut in and whisked her away.

Cam tried to use the time as the wedding wound down to come up with a plan. He needed a good one.

THE LAST OF the guests were locating their cars when Adair slipped away to her office. She needed a moment to think. Barry and Rexie were going to stay in Glen Loch in a bed-and-breakfast. She'd arranged that right after she'd made a call to Reverend Foley. And they were going to talk about their future. Before they'd left the stone arch, they'd been talking about perhaps spending part of the year in Montana and part in New York.

The important thing was that they were talking. Nerves jittered in her stomach. They'd been dancing around there ever since Cam had told her they needed to talk. And he was looking for her even now.

Adair sank into her chair and dropped her head in her hands. She knew what he wanted to talk about. They'd made a deal. They would enjoy each other until his work here was done. And it was. Scalzo and his partner were under arrest and her wedding problem was solved. The fat lady had sung.

And she'd gotten just what she wanted—her Sutherland fantasy fling.

Unless you do something about it.

Lifting her head, she looked at the metal box. Then she tore a yellow sheet of paper off of a legal pad and wrote down what she really wanted before she placed it with her other dreams and fantasies. Maybe it was time she tapped into that power again. Grabbing the box, she hurried out of her office.

AFTER SEARCHING EVERYWHERE, Cam found her in the stone arch on her hands and knees. The moment he called her name, she rose and turned. As he walked toward her, the nerves that had been skittering through his system all afternoon intensified. She was the only woman who'd ever made him feel this way. The only one he'd ever wanted to plan for. To plan with.

He just had to pray that he could sell his plan to her.

The air was perfumed with flowers and moonlight gleamed in a bright path across the lake as he joined her beneath the stone arch. For just a moment, Cam had the feeling that they were not alone. He thought of all the couples through all the years who'd stood right where they were standing and who'd found what the legend promised. Looking into Adair's eyes, he knew he wanted what they'd wanted.

"I want to talk to you about us," he began.

Adair felt something tighten around her heart. Maybe she'd tapped out all the power by getting her fantasy fling.

"Things have happened very fast between us."

She couldn't seem to get a breath. He was going to say that they'd had a great time and now he had to go back with Daryl to D.C. and she would have to get ready for the next wedding. He'd be in touch. And he probably wouldn't be.

She didn't want to hear it. "I know what you're going to say. You have to go back with Daryl. You'll be in touch, but—"

"No. Yes." He took her other hand, gripped both of them hard. "Don't put words in my mouth. I'm having enough trouble finding the ones I want on my own. I've tried all day to come up with a plan. And I'm really lousy at this."

"A plan?" She stared at him.

"There hasn't been enough time. I want more…I need more…."

"Time for what?" Then, because she saw some of the turmoil she was feeling in his eyes, she shut up.

Cam took a deep breath and let it out. "I want more time with you. I need more time to—I want to be able to give you your fantasy."

"My fantasy?" Baffled, she stared at him. "Is that some kind of CIA code I'm supposed to crack?"

"No." He released her hands to grip her shoulders. "I'm speaking in plain English. Here's the plan. I want to give you your secret fantasy. I just need more time."

She stared at him. "My secret—"

Then she suddenly got it. She pushed his hands away and then used her own to give him a shove hard enough to send him stumbling back against the wall. "You read what was in that metal box, didn't you? How could you?"

"I'm a CIA agent. I'm curious. And I wanted to know more about you. Dammit, I've been wanting to know more about you since I was ten. And I think I fell in love with you the day our parents got married."

Because her legs had gone suddenly weak, Adair sat down on the ledge that ran along one side of the arch.

"Well?" Cam asked.

For a moment, she couldn't speak. He looked angry. And stunned. She could sympathize with the latter. "That's what you wanted to talk to me about? That you fell in love with me seven years ago?"

"No. I came out here to tell you about my plan. Just because I'm in D.C. and you're here doesn't mean that we can't spend time together." He waved a hand. "I was thinking long weekends. Once we get the security beefed up here. We still don't know who's been visiting the library." He was starting to babble. He never babbled. "I know you like to look at the big picture. And you can feel free to fill in the details."

When she simply stared at him, he paced to the far end of the arch, then walked back. He never paced, either. He was good at improvising, and he was blowing this. Panic bubbled up. "Look, I don't know why or how this happened, but you're right for me. And I want to be the one who gives you your fantasy. The only one. Because you *are* my fantasy. You're everything. Clear enough?"

She studied him for a moment as everything inside of her melted. He was standing there, scowling at her, and the tension inside of her completely eased. Cam preferred to go with the flow, act on impulse. It was one of the things she liked about him. Loved about him. But he'd tried to make a plan for her. And as odd as it seemed, he was right for her, too. He was just simply right for her. And she wanted him forever. That's what she'd written on the yellow paper she'd just buried in the stones.

Rising, she moved toward him. "About this plan—is it a five-year one or longer?"

He studied her for a moment and she could see the tension flow out of him, too. "Longer."

She put her hands on his face and drew it down to hers. "How much longer?"

He was smiling as he lowered his mouth to hers. "I think it's going to take me quite a while to fulfill your fantasies."

"But you did say I could fill in the details. So when you finish, I'm going to start on your fantasies."

He laughed as he drew her in close and held her tight. "That will take a lot of time," he promised. "I have a lot of them. And I'll be making up new ones as we go along."

"Sounds like a plan," Adair said.

They were laughing as they sank to their knees beneath the stone arch that Angus One had built for his true love.

"Tell me again that you love me," she said when his lips were nearly brushing hers.

"I love you, Adair."

"Here's another detail. I love you, too."

And when Cam covered her mouth with his, a whisper of wind sighed across the stones.

* * * * *

A sneaky peek at next month...

Blaze®

SCORCHING HOT, SEXY READS

My wish list for next month's titles...

In stores from 17th August 2012:

☐ Cowboy Up – Vicki Lewis Thompson

& No Going Back – Karen Foley

☐ Tall, Dark & Reckless – Heather MacAllister

& No Holds Barred – Cara Summers

Available at WHSmith, Tesco, Asda, Eason, Amazon and Apple

Just can't wait?

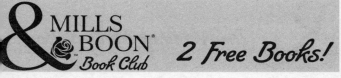

MILLS & BOON® Book Club

2 Free Books!

Get your free books now at
www.millsandboon.co.uk/freebookoffer

Or fill in the form below and post it back to us

THE MILLS & BOON® BOOK CLUB™—HERE'S HOW IT WORKS: Accepting your free books places you under no obligation to buy anything. You may keep the books and return the despatch note marked 'Cancel'. If we do not hear from you, about a month later we'll send you 4 brand-new stories from the Blaze® series, including a 2-in-1 book priced at £5.49 and two single books priced at £3.49* each. There is no extra charge for post and packaging. You may cancel at any time, otherwise we will send you 4 stories a month which you may purchase or return to us—the choice is yours. *Terms and prices subject to change without notice. Offer valid in UK only. Applicants must be 18 or over. Offer expires 31st January 2013. **For full terms and conditions, please go to www.millsandboon.co.uk/freebookoffer**

Mrs/Miss/Ms/Mr (please circle) _____

First Name _____

Surname _____

Address _____

_____

_____ Postcode _____

E-mail _____

Send this completed page to: Mills & Boon Book Club, Free Book Offer, FREEPOST NAT 10298, Richmond, Surrey, TW9 1BR

Find out more at
www.millsandboon.co.uk/freebookoffer

Visit us Online

0712/K2YEA

The World of Mills & Boon®

There's a Mills & Boon® series that's perfect for you. We publish ten series and, with new titles every month, you never have to wait long for your favourite to come along.

Blaze.

Scorching hot, sexy reads
4 new stories every month

By Request

Relive the romance with the best of the best
9 new stories every month

Cherish

Romance to melt the heart every time
12 new stories every month

Desire

Passionate and dramatic love stories
8 new stories every month

Special Offers

Every month we put together collections and longer reads written by your favourite authors.

Here are some of next month's highlights— and don't miss our fabulous discount online!

On sale 17th August

On sale 7th September

On sale 7th September

Save 20%
on all Special Releases